MW00466868

QUENCH THE SMOLDERING

WICK

Gordon Peter Wilson

Book layout and cover design by Carter Wilson

TO: ANDREW + SUSU

A bruised reed He will not break and a smoldering wick He will not quench until He brings forth justice to victory.

Matthew 12:20 from Isaiah 42:3

Table
Of Contents

Chapter 1
Sweatsplash

THE IRONY OF HAVING TO BUY HIS mistress a Mercedes-Benz was not lost on 64-year old Shale Gimmel. Truth be told in Gath, the name originated as Gimmel*farb*, but his great-grandfather gently shed the cumbersome extremity in transition from a first-generation Jewish peddler to established dry goods proprietor, just as New Orleans itself made the transition from wholesale exchange terminus to post-industrial, bourgeois metropolis. Gimmel*farb* was just *too* Jewish, and the idea was to blend in with the Americans. Now four generations later, Shale continued the tradition of cosmetic assimilation when he willingly submitted to his twin daughters' inevitable, yet understandable, demand for dual nose jobs. At a certain age, the Gimmel girls had come to realize that certain physical characteristics of their heritage might, like their former family name, present an impediment to their social and romantic aspiration. The miracle of modern surgery had outstripped the power of evolution itself, at least (if only temporarily) in time for the Junior-Senior prom. *How goodly are thy rhinoplasties, O Israel!* And to think, after all that, he was in the market for a Mercedes — for his gentile concubine! It was just unimaginable to Shale.

The name, thus pruned to Gimmel, still lacked the mellifluous cadence of the early Sephardic surnames of the earliest New Orleans Jews (Toledano, Monsanto, de Pass, Delgado, de Oliveira, Solis or Touro) or the aristocratic *cachet* of very early German-Jewish New Orleans names (Stern, Lemann, Weis, Marx or Steeg) or the equally Mandarin Biblical names (Israel, Benjamin, Moses, Simon or Levy). But it was an effective foreshortening of a distended *Ashkenazi* identifier. In that sense, Shale was forever preoccupied with ways to shave off some of his ethnic *Hebraica*, to scrape off some of the pickle-barrel *yid* that made him so self-consciously Jewish. Shale resented this chronic anxiety and the older New Orleans Jewish families (known as "St. Charles Avenue Jews") who superciliously harbored a condescension toward Eastern European Jews and their descendants who had, because of their strange customs and ancient, alien raiment, undone the nearly complete assimilation seamlessly achieved by their New Orleans coreligionists in the early part of the 20th century. (The *Sephardim* with their elegiac, Aristotelian ease of assimilation! The bastards!) Shale had been aware all his life that the sudden ship borne arrival of Russian and Polish Jews in New Orleans at the turn of the century had distressed the viziers of the established German-Jewish families. They tried shipping off the fuzzy mongrels to Catahoula Parish, promising them a life of freedom and comfort on subsidized farms, but that didn't take. The *Ostjuden* weren't very good farmers to begin with, and the irresistible draw of the mercantile trades, to which they were accustomed abroad, ultimately deposited them in the ghettoes of balkanized New Orleans. It was then that an uneasy Jewish co-existence began and a mutual resentment found its nascence – a resentment that was to remain mostly hidden from preoccupied Edwardian New Orleans society.

No, Shale would remind himself, this resentment was positively not for *goyische* consumption. For the most part, the sublimated mistrust was kept within the Faith because being inconspicuous was the best defense against what was, in New Orleans until the 1920s, only latent anti-Semitism. Shale was always careful to honor the unspoken rule among Jews that the tension between the two factions was to remain hidden — better for everyone that the matter remain *sub rosa*.

There was at least one uncomfortable instance, however, in Shale's childhood when this awkward struggle surfaced for all the world to see, and Shale knew it well. In the winter of 1960, the Civic Theatre scheduled a local première of the film *Exodus*: a dramatization of the birth and emergence of the State of Israel in the late 1940s. It was not exactly radical

Zionist propaganda, but its message did not sit well with certain elements of the reactionary right, particularly the American Nazi party. The leader of that group, George Lincoln Rockwell, had called upon all like-minded neo-Nazis and anti-Semites from across the American South to storm the theater on the night of the film's debut. The most recent wave of Jewish immigrants to New Orleans, concentration camp victims and refugees from Hitler's Final Solution, referred to as "New Americans," got extremely agitated and threatened to obstruct the Nazi sympathizers with physical force. The westernized Jewish gentry of New Orleans, by that time fully assimilated but still careful to remain as inconspicuous as possible, summoned all their resources to dampen the muscular righteousness of the New Americans. Mollification and appeasement presented the only sensible approach. *Fregnicht! Zugnicht! Keep a low profile!* The St. Charles Avenue Jews had come too far to let an impassioned minority resuscitate an expired European conflict on the streets of New Orleans. These divergent interests caused a great deal of consternation within the Jewish community, especially for the established German-Jewish bourgeoisie who did not want to magnify any Jewish ethnicity by allowing expressions of outrage or threats of disruption by the New Americans and their natural confederates, the *Ostjuden*.

This uneasiness was not an abstraction to Shale. His own marriage was a demonstrable example: an imbalance of power between his wife, an old-line Jewish aristocrat (if there could be such a thing) and him, a third-generation descendant of Orthodox Jews who had married up. His wife never held it over on him or used it as blackmail to finish a quarrel, but he could still feel it. In fact, he was aware of it at all times, not just when interacting with his wife, but in everyday business dealings and social occasions, an inseparable part of his personality, his constitution, even as far back as childhood.

Shale retained vivid boyhood memories of attending Yiddish-speaking meetings with his father at Ralph Rosenblat's butcher shop on Carondelet Street (a street near the main Dryades Street thoroughfare of an Orthodox Jewish neighborhood known as "Little

Warsaw"). Discussions were often heated and he admired his father for expressing solidarity with those who would reject calls for non-confrontation and appeasement espoused by the St. Charles Avenue Jews. And so, Shale's resentment toward the pusillanimous Jewish establishment began at an early age.

Even still, this unsettled political dysphoria was not, especially now, for public display, though Shale secretly fantasized that he could at any time drag things down to the *shtetl* should the Dutchtown paladins display the slightest suggestion of pharisaical *hauteur*. His readiness to humble those who had foresworn their ethno-Jewishness was not religiously motivated. Religion, Shale often thought, was for women and children. His resentment was personal.

Shale Gimmel's family business, now known as Gimmex, Inc., started as a general store with capital accumulated by his great-grandfather Jacob Gimmelfarb (born in Poland or Upper Silesia or Lithuania or some such place) from foreclosures on promissory notes given by poor white tenant farmers and Negroes in return for manufactured goods unavailable in the very rural stretches of south and southwest Louisiana. Security for those promissory notes was often farmland, acreage that Jacob was able to bundle and sell higgledy-piggledy as economic opportunity manifested. Over the span of four generations, Gimmelfarb's General Store had grown into Gimmex, Inc., a commercial food supply behemoth serving the entire Gulf South and now worth well over three-quarters of $1 billion. Shale often took solace in this financial security when put under stress and it served its purpose at times like this when he was practically being blackmailed into buying his mistress a German sports car.

Nevertheless, she was a perfect mistress, with perfect tits, a tiny nose and slender hips made for low-rise jeans. Her name was Kristen Duplechain (or was it Kirsten? he could never get that straight) and she was from Destrehan, Louisiana, a semi-rural suburb of New Orleans where his great-grandfather once peddled wares out of a canvas sack and where the largest slave insurrection in American history had erupted in the early 1800s. "Kiddo," as he had taken to calling her since he could not remember her name, was a paralegal at one of the old-line New Orleans law firms on the 35th floor of a salmon-colored, post-modern office tower on Poydras Street, constructed on the very site where his great-grandfather's general store originally stood — another irony not lost on 64-year-old Shale Gimmel. The law firm, Stein, Mayer and Beer was founded in the 1920s by scions of that same snooty German-Jewish nobility he resented. He often consciously relished having plucked out one of their female employees for his recreational concupiscence.

Shale originally met Kiddo at a VIP reception for premium season-ticket holders of New Orleans' NBA team, the Corsairs. Kiddo was a former member of the team's dance squad, the Corvettes, and now served as a brand ambassadress for the organization. She and her sister sirens wined and dined older men susceptible to flirtation and already giddy being associated with pro sports, basketball in particular. Shale loved professional basketball, though he could not say exactly why. Was there something in his Jewishness that made basketball so enjoyable?

Perhaps, Shale often considered, it was the same phenomenon at work in the Catskills when, in the 1940s and 50s, New York Jews spent their summers watching the Negro waiters from Grossinger's Hotel and Zalkin's play basketball at an outdoor court set up at Kutsher's Country Club. There had to be a genetic predisposition for Shale's love of basketball, something inveterate, but he never could completely comprehend it.

Shale's love for basketball was similar to his preference for modern, abstract art over traditional realism — there was something in his DNA that attracted him to the Abstract Expressionists of the 1920s New York School — artists with familiar and comforting names like Gottlieb, Hoffman, Krasner, Newman, Rothko(witz), and Leon Golub. These artists were probably already drawn to abstraction as radicals, Shale figured, but a similar atavism must have found a perfect pretext in the sacred proscription against figurative art in Hebrew scripture, an ancient law from the Book of Isaiah forbidding the realistic depiction of any living thing in the sea or under the sun. Shale's attraction to abstract art was irresistible and he considered all other art forms inferior. There was, of course, one exception to this rule (abstract art only!) that Shale very naturally recognized: the Social Realism of artists like Ben Shahn, Jack Levine, William Gropper and Phillip Evergood — Lithuanian and Polish Jews of the New York Art Students League who, as occasional contributors to the communist periodical *Morning Freiheit* and other leftist publications Shale's father collected, made the human form the centerpiece of their collective *oeuvre.* (Arthur Szyk, because he was a *mere* illustrator, occupied a special place in Shale's album of acceptable artists, and needless to say, Romare Bearden, Horace Pippen and Jacob Lawrence because they were black.) Depictions of labor union delegates proselytizing on soapboxes and blue-collar workers spooning soup were altogether suitable for the discrete chambers of Shale's overwrought aesthetic. All of these predilections seemed to spring from his chromosomes, a trilling wire in his blood played to the tune of a *Misheberach* lament in a *Freygish* musical scale. Suffering, contrition, compassion, despair.

Of course, Shale's support for labor unions was axiomatic. On the other hand, Gimmex, Inc. was a non-union operation inasmuch as Louisiana was a right-to-work state and because his employees had no need for labor unions: Shale ensured that they were flush with health benefits, competitive wages and day care, and, as he liked to say, *for other reasons too complicated to get into,* which really meant *I don't in fact have any more reasons but if I fob it all off as an enumerative nuisance, no one will be any the wiser*. Shale knew precisely what Karl Marx meant when he wrote of those who live lives of private privilege and practical necessity.

Figurative art, therefore, that promoted union interests overrode any Talmudic prohibition. After all, Shale would remind himself, Ida Kohlmeyer herself slipped in a figurative representation of an androgynous child to her stained-glass mural for the Touro Synagogue Chapel Annex on St. Charles Avenue. Leon Golub sidestepped the same prescription when he designed another stained-glass window for a synagogue in Chicago in the 1960s that depicted the human form of Joseph. Shale could also remember that an enterprising rabbi had rooted through the *Talmud* to find a scholarly validation for permitting slugger Hank Greenberg to play a baseball game on Rosh Hoshanna when the Detroit Tigers were locked in a pennant race in the 1930s. If Ida Kohlmeyer and Hank Greenberg could make an exception, so could he. Besides, he couldn't help it. There were certain things about American culture he couldn't resist. Basketball and modern art were delightful diversions, to say nothing of that other great American tradition afforded men of great wealth: the mistress. Perhaps if he looked hard enough, he could find Talmudic approbation for that luxury as well.

Sex with Kiddo Duplechain was never love, but it was magnificent. Though she would not let him kiss her with his tongue, she was game for everything else, certainly a lot more than the physical contact he had with his wife. He married his wife Millie, born Magda Adler, to an assimilated Jewish family well-entrenched in the old-line, all-Jewish Harmony Club (modeled after New York's *Gesselschaft Harmonie,* itself established as a social organization for westernized German Jews denied admittance to the Union Club), when he was 24 and she 22. She was, at the time, a genuine lover, though she no longer made him feel like a Maccabean guerilla or an Italian race car driver. But Millie had given him the twins upon whom he lavished a fatherly tenderness that his millions could never express. Their names were Caroline and Lindsey. Shale and Millie agonized over the naming of these two babies (under intense pressure from the mother-in-law who always disapproved of her daughter's marriage to an *Ostjuden* peasant like Shale) and settled at last on the most Episcopalian sounding names they could cull from the yearbooks of Trinity Episcopal School. They couldn't get away with quintessentially New Orleans *pompon* names like "Coco," "Gigi," "Susu," "Mimi," "Cici" or "Fifi," but Caroline and Lindsey somehow seemed workable.

The real irony was that Trinity School stood on a lot once occupied by the mansion of Julius Weis, a

German Jewish patriarch and cotton broker who was one of the last Jewish members of the Boston Club, New Orleans' most prestigious and (now exclusively) Anglo-Saxon men's club. It was the immigration of Eastern European Jews to New Orleans that put an end to Jewish membership in the Boston Club and was the main source of resentment that bubbled up within the Jewish community from time to time in awkward, social or, in the case of the *Exodus* incident, political situations. The fact that Trinity School now stood on and around the property where the stately Julius Weis home once stood gave Shale a special sort of satisfaction and yet, at the same time, revulsion. At any rate, Caroline and Lindsey were the names they settled on. He and his wife had considered spelling it "Lindsay," "Lindsy," or "Lindsie", but they decided to play it straight. The spelling of "Caroline," of course, was untouchable, the *summa cognomen* of the Episcopalian firmament, a Hobden of the old unaltered blood, imbued with a sacrosanct Hanoverian majesty that was strictly reserved for the first female child. It was a name not to be tinkered with. It could not be

"Carolyn", "Carolina" or, even worse, "Carol," the 1970's suburban Midwest Tupperwife who shopped at Baker's Discount Department Store and lusted for her dentist. No, Shale knew that he and Millie were pretenders, wealthy and confident, but pretenders nonetheless, laying an audacious claim to a red velvet heraldry largely unknown to ordinary Jews. For some strange reason, Catholics never named their daughters "Caroline" either, which came as something of a relief to Shale and Millie, who were putting as much distance as they could between themselves and all things ethnic. The name "Caroline" had become a *shibboleth* that allowed access to a very exclusive club — superficially, at least. Shale was learning from Millie the effectiveness of these little details. Assimilation could be a delicate bit of embroidery.

But Shale would have loved the twins just as much had they named them after matriarchs of the Hebrew Bible like Sarah or Leah or Rebecca or Rachel, but that was not going to happen. He, at the insistence of his wife, had gotten into the assimilation game and there was no turning back. There were other Jewish families who felt enough time had passed to begin a campaign to establish traditional Hebrew names on the rosters of mainstream society legitimacy, but Shale and Millie were not quite ready to take up the cause. They wanted to *fit in.*

On this hot September morning, Shale stood at the kitchen counter in his Garden District home pretending to leaf through mail his wife had thoughtfully and carefully placed in the slots of an antique silver English toast rack for his review. Though his eyes were fixed downward as the fingers of his right hand flicked one envelope after another to the back of the deck he held in the palm of his left hand, his mind was racing. His wife, Millie, sat at the kitchen table scribbling something on a loose-leaf pad. She looked peaceful and pretty for her age, and it almost broke Shale's heart to do what he was about to do: start a fake fight. It would be a cheap, facile and churlish thing to do, but it was expedient. If you are going to cheat on your wife, you have to ratchet up a superficially moral justification to dampen the guilt, and a domestic argument, even a manufactured one, was just the thing.

Shale spoke.

"Did you arrange a Sweet Sixteen Party group for the girls like I asked you?"

"I'm trying. They're trying to get in with the right group. Everything is so clique-ish at that age," explained Millie. "Money doesn't carry the same weight in the Sweet Sixteen circuit as it does with the grownups."

"What's that supposed to mean?" snapped Shale, finding his footing.

"What's what supposed to mean?"

"I suppose we're considered *nouveau riche* interlopers trying to muscle in with a swish set."

"No! No!" said Millie, obviously sensing that Shale was spoiling for a fight. "The girls are being as gentle as possible with their friends trying to put together the best group!"

"I suppose you think an old Polish Jew like me prevents our children from enjoying the privileges you and your St. Charles Avenue family feel entitled." Shale was warming to his pernicious task.

"No! Not at all!" said Millie, bleating.

Shale interrupted: "I can just hear your Mother's condescension in your own voice. It never stops with you. I'm to blame any time your social climbing hits a snag. I'm sick of it." Shale feared, suddenly, that his staged indignation had accelerated too quickly. Millie tried to lower the temperature:

"Shale! Please, darling, that has nothing to do with it! They're just teenagers who…"

A guilty feeling began to descend on Shale and he reasoned that he should mercifully end the unpleasantness. He had, after all, accomplished what he set out to accomplish.

"Typical of you to be passive-aggressive about it." Shale was not sure what that meant, but it was a perfect omnibus petard he could lob at his wife and daisycut any quibbling defenses she might, however meekly, offer up as a predicate to his choreographed, melodramatic storm-off. And so, he stormed off — to his study to gather his suit coat and car keys, leaving Millie close to tears. Shale was ashamed, but if she ever caught him cheating he could say that it shouldn't be surprising, that they were growing apart anyway.

Having an affair was hard work, distasteful in more ways than one.

All of this was unfortunate, but it was over, and it was time to turn his attention to the matter at hand: the purchase, or, to be more precise, lease, of a white Mercedes-Benz C250 Coupe for his girlfriend, who was herself being *leased*, so to speak. Shale had devoted his lunch hour to this project and was driving his silver Cadillac XTS sedan down Tulane Avenue to meet Kiddo and her two housemates, Angela Waguespack and Trisha Chauvin at Monaco Motor Cars where his trusted salesman and *confidante*, Joey Giambelluca, was ready to make delivery. The black leather interior of his Cadillac was sleek and sumptuous, although at the time he chose that option he neglected to consider New Orleans' September heat. The black upholstery never seemed to cool down no matter how ferociously the air conditioner was blowing. The perspiration forming on his brow and cheek was making it difficult to apply the small amount of base pancake makeup his vanity demanded whenever a tryst with Kiddo was in the offing.

Beginning at age 60, his cheeks had begun to display a capillary *craqueleur* that the pancake makeup seemed to disguise. Still, beads of sweat continued to seep through the cosmetic application and he wondered whether sex with Kiddo was worth all the trouble. That internal argument was over almost before it began. As he pondered his physical relationship with Kiddo, Shale was suddenly struck with the sinking feeling that can ruin any man's sense of equanimity: Demon Embarrassment.

As it happened, three weeks earlier, Shale had arranged a tryst with Kiddo at his most recent acquisition: a hotel. On the advice of his ambitious research and development staff, he had purchased and renovated the former Pontchartrain Hotel on St. Charles Avenue on the edge of the old Dryades Street neighborhood where he lived as a young boy and where the Orthodox Eastern European Jewish community, including the Gimmelfarb clan, had congregated when they first immigrated to New Orleans. The Pontchartrain Hotel building was designed by the venerable architectural firm of Weiss, Dreyfus, Inc., a nationally if not internationally famous outfit responsible for designing the Louisiana State Capitol in Baton Rouge, the Bradford Furniture Warehouse on Howard Avenue and many other architectural landmarks of Louisiana.

The Weiss, Dreyfous firm was a troubled but enormously productive partnership between Leon Weiss, the ambitious descendant of an itinerant Polish peddler who had migrated to New Orleans from rural, northern Louisiana before World War I, and his eventual brother-in-law, Julius Dreyfous, the anointed son of one of the oldest and most assimilated Alsatian Jewish families of the city. Shale knew that the two families held a mutual, lingering resentment that began during the Huey P. Long era when Leon Weiss was indicted for submitting fictitious change orders to the Louisiana Board of Regents involving the construction of state government buildings. Leon was Long's captive architect-laureate, his Albert Speer, and he could not seem to avoid associating with the malefactors of the Long political machine. The Weiss family felt that Leon had nobly taken the fall for the firm and that Julius Dreyfous had put forth no effort to assist in his brother-in-law's criminal defense. The Dreyfous family remained largely silent on this ticklish family embarrassment as they were privately embittered by the confirmation that their concerns about Leon's *mechula* breeding had proven out. From the beginning of the courtship between Caroline Dreyfous and Leon Weiss, the Dreyfous family suspected Leon was insinuating himself in the aristocratic organism of their family. After all, the Benjamins spoke only to the Dreyfouses, and the Dreyfouses spoke only to God. They did not intend for a tramp-class parvenu like Leon Weiss to compromise their place in that hierarchy. Julius Dreyfous even tried to sabotage his sister's engagement to Leon by disclosing Leon's first marriage to a woman who died under suspicious circumstances, as well as Leon's dalliance with a disreputable floozy after his wife's death. The Dreyfous clan ultimately accepted the marriage begrudgingly but the tension within the firm, even after they became relatives by marriage, never eased. After Leon was released from prison, Julius

Dreyfous wanted nothing more to do with him. Shale naturally sided with the Weiss family considering their mutual *yiddishkeit* backgrounds. To think that he had purchased a hotel designed by two men on opposite ends of the New Orleans Jewish social spectrum struck Shale as slightly ironic. He and his own wife were living out an identical arrangement.

At any rate, the New York City design firm, de Stijl, persuaded Shale to name the hotel "The Watercress" after the indigenous Louisiana leaf vegetable that grows almost anywhere water flows in the American tropics. Not "The Watercress Hotel" and not "Hotel Watercress," for those stylistic affectations had gone stale. No, it was simply to be "The Watercress" and the ground floor restaurant would simply be called "Moss." Not "The Moss Room" or "Restaurant Moss" just "Moss." At first, Shale bristled at the names suggested by the imagineers at de Stijl, ignorant as they were that the name "Moss" was the name of another old-line Jewish family in New Orleans that he did not intend to flatter. He was ultimately disabused of that concern, so the name "Moss," along with "The Watercress," made its hospitality industry debut. Varying shades of the color green were to be the hotel's *motif* and everything from stationery to pillow shams to carpeting would carry the theme. Antique pottery from 1920's Sophie Newcomb College would complete the effect.

But Demon Embarrassment interrupted these thoughts and made herself comfortable. On the earlier trysting occasion he could not shake from his memory, Shale and Kiddo had met in the Melon Suite of The Watercress and, after the usual compulsory preliminaries, he proceeded to fuck her in the missionary position. She on her back and he with his torso jacked up at an angle by his locked elbows, they began the squirm, throb and thrust of sexual congress. Ten minutes into this primordial exercise, Shale allowed himself a brief glance at the point of penetration. How disappointed he was to see only the crispy thicket of his salt and pepper pubic hair mashing into the glabrous ivory pate of her pelvic saddle horn. So dense and overgrown was his pubic foliage that he could not see his member making the plunge. But he could feel it. And it was literally sensational. But just as the pleasure chemicals in his bloodstream had started to release, he could feel a substantial droplet of perspiration forming on the tip of his nose. His nose! That bio-racial extremity 5000 years in the making was now to be the flashpoint of his *un*making! That globule of sweat, suffused with all the supersaturated salinity of the Dead Sea, was beginning to relent. He could feel the tensile strength of the semi-liquid droplet, an emulsion of bodily fluid and pancake makeup, weaken. But, being so close to the finish, he could not stop and risk losing all the ground he had covered. So, just as he came to climax, the droplet abandoned its clutches and splashed on the apple of the cheek of his defenseless mistress.

At that instant, the erotic mood vanished. Kiddo wriggled out from underneath him in horrified disgust. As he rolled onto his elbow in an attempt to be accommodating, Shale watched her scamper naked toward the bathroom to cleanse and disinfect. He immediately knew that this disgusting misfortune was going to cost him. He didn't know that it was going to cost him a white Mercedes-Benz C250 Coupe, but, after some uncomfortable negotiation, that was the compensation they settled on. And so, Kristen (or Kirsten?) Duplechain, her two roommates, Angela Waguespack and Trisha Chauvin, sat in the customers' lounge of Monaco Motor Cars, under the supervision of trusted Joey Giambelluca, awaiting Shale Gimmel and his checkbook.

Upon arrival, Shale checked his makeup one last time, strode through the plate glass door and into the customers' lounge.

"Mr. Shale!" cried the dependable car salesman, Joey. "I think we're all set."

Kiddo and her two Cajun roommates stood up and surrounded him fawningly with semi-affectionate caresses. To Angela and Trisha, he gave cheek-to-cheek kisses of acknowledgment, and to Kiddo, he extended his two flat, cantilevered, leathery lips to the tightly pursed flower of her mouth, the only oral contact, such as it was, she would permit him. It was just like the kisses Shale had seen Hugh Hefner give his live-in girlfriends on that reality television show.

"Joey has the white coupe pulled up right out front," said Kiddo in triumph. "It's got the tan leather interior that we talked about."

"I hope you found this one on the lot," quipped Shale, in mock seriousness, "or else this little beauty's gonna put me in the poor house."

"Don't you worry Mr. Shale. It's all like we discussed. Everything included. The number never changed," said Joey, reassuringly, trying to dampen any developing uneasiness.

Shale made a suggestion: "Why don't you girls go for a spin while Joey and I talk business?"

"Good idea," said Kiddo.

"We'll go pick up some daiquiris and hot guys," said Angela attempting some playful levity. As the girls walked away arm in arm, Shale caught them whispering and giggling as if they were being set free to hit the town and impress some *real* boyfriends. Could Kiddo be involved with someone else? She was a young, attractive girl with a lot of free time away from Shale and his family life. It would really piss him off if he found out she intended to seduce a man closer to *her* age with *his* car. He must watch the situation closely.

As the girls drove off on their impish errand, Shale and Joey marched to the salesman's cubicle to do manly, grown-up things. As they walked, Shale surveyed Joey's classic salesman's outfit as Joey made small talk about his progress towards a law degree taking night classes at Loyola University School of Law.

"I just finished my second year. I'll be a 3L this year. My Con Crim Pro exam was tough, but they say Loyola's got the best Con Crim Pro program in the country," boasted Joey, oblivious to the fact that Shale knew nothing of constitutional criminal procedure, by its abbreviated nickname or otherwise. Nevertheless, Shale became vaguely aware of Joey's unspoken message. Shale had noticed that Loyola people, especially in the presence of Tulane people, harbored a kind of inferiority complex when it came to their school. Shale was a Tulane graduate and he now sat on the Board of Governors, particular facts that Joey was well aware of, though Shale had never mentioned them to him. For some reason, Loyola people resented the way they thought Tulane people, and New Orleanians at large, looked down on them. They bristled at the fact that Loyola was considered a less prestigious institution than Tulane and were forever campaigning to rehabilitate Loyola's image as a second-tier academic institution. Shale had often overheard Loyola people privately soliciting prospective subscribers to disparage Tulane by appealing to a presumed sense of anti-Semitism as a cover for the real source of their resentment: image inadequacy. They would beseech, as if to say, "Come one, come all! Join me in my contempt for Tulane, for they are 'The Jews!'" never letting on that they envied the elevated academic reputation enjoyed, deservedly or not, by Tulane. Shale, himself, never really thought about it, but if you had asked him in his undergraduate days what he thought about Loyola, he would have said that Loyola was a fine little college for working class Catholics living down their vegetable cart legacies. It was like asking him what he thought about Shreveport or Canada — it never occurred to him to formulate an opinion. Perhaps, Shale often considered, this was the image Loyola people were trying to recast.

As he reflected upon Joey's clumsy stratagem, Shale once again took an inventory of Joey's clothing: Loyola Wolfpack maroon dress shirt, floral print tie, black, triple-pleated slacks with thin cuffs, black-and-tan slip-on loafers with basket weave uppers and tassels. He looked like a homicide detective. His fat feet caused the loafers to bulge outward over the flattened shoe soles. He looked to Shale like he stepped right out of the display window of Joe Gemelli's Men's Wear on Camp Street in the 1980's. Sicilians had emigrated to New Orleans about the same time that his ancestors came from Eastern Europe, but Shale wondered why they could never wipe away their immigrant *patina*. They didn't even change their names to seem less ethnic. But all of this was beside the point. Shale was anxious to get the lease agreement signed and to put the sweatsplash episode behind him. Besides, his friend and associate, David Kaminsky, the president of Tulane University, had called an emergency Board of Governors meeting to discuss a volatile development that was threatening to disrupt the beginning of Tulane's fall semester: The Asian American Students Union was protesting the use of the word "orientation" in the official "New Student Orientation Program," an innocently named welcoming event provided by the University to acclimate incoming students to a college campus life they would be experiencing for the first time. Something had to be done administratively because President Kaminsky feared that things were about to turn ugly.

Chapter 2

Pigeontown

EARLIER THAT MORNING, ON THE same day that Shale Gimmel was negotiating the lease of a white Mercedes-Benz sports car for his mistress, Jupiter Mingo strolled through his Pigeontown neighborhood, just three or four miles from Monaco Motor Cars. He paused before a small, glass-fronted bookcase mounted on the Leonidas Street curbside, just one block from the residence on Monroe Street he rented from Mrs. Josephine Boniface who lived in the other half of the shotgun double. The bookcase was part of a New Orleans city program known as Little Free Library. In an attempt to bring whatever literature it could to the poor black sections of the city, the mayor's office, with the cooperation of the New Orleans Public Library, installed a dozen or so miniature outdoor bookcases stocked with paperbacks that any citizen could check out. As far as Jupiter knew, nobody but him ever took advantage of the service.

Jupiter Mingo was 28 years old, clean shaven (unusual, he knew, for a black man) with medium-length dreadlocks. He had dropped out of school in the 10th grade, but continued his education on his own. Jupiter took to independent study as a form of liberation. His intellectual esurience grew as he learned, and one research project seemed to lead to the next. As he got better at it, reading transported him. In his imagination he could travel without limitation and investigate any amusing curiosity. Proficiency with language meant efficiency of expression and understanding. He began to draw parallels between historical events separated by generations and theorize about their origins and consequences. The subject matter he pursued was widely varied, sometimes esoteric but always fresh, at least to him. Nothing interested him more, however, than local, sociological history and its immediate, practical application to his everyday life. This kind of research naturally drew him to the neighborhood's Little Free Library where non-fiction books by regional publishing houses about local subjects often seemed to find their way.

Just as Jupiter began to browse through the modest offering of paperbacks on that hot September morning, a blue and white police cruiser with lights flashing (but no siren) approached. A short, squat, white patrolman got out and walked toward Jupiter as he stood before the book stand. The cop wore a thick leather utility belt around his carbohydrate waist that squeaked each time he adjusted it with his pink thumbs. "Here we go," thought Jupiter. "Time for some routine, light harassment." "What's on your mind, my man?" asked the corpulent officer.

"What's on my mind?" Jupiter asked. "Minding my own business is what's on my mind."

"Let's see some identification."

"Have I done something wrong?"

"Step over here," said the cop, noticeably bracing for trouble. "You fellas don't generally carry identification, do you?"

"What's the problem, officer?" asked Jupiter, trying not to act rattled.

"The only problem we have is that you ain't showing me no identification."

Jupiter sensed that it was time to offer at least passive cooperation. "I've got identification. But I don't see any reason for this."

"Let's have it," said the officer. Jupiter extracted his wallet from his pants pocket and produced one blue and white paper card and one laminated yellow card.

"What is this?" asked the officer.

"It's my Social Security card and my New Orleans Public Library card."

"Where's your driver's license?"

"I don't have a driver's license. I don't drive."

"Sit down on the curb right here." While walking back to his police cruiser, the officer examined the two identification cards Jupiter had produced. He watched as the officer squeezed into the front seat of the cruiser and pressed the transmit button on his shoulder-mounted police radio microphone and began to speak. Jupiter couldn't hear anything except intermittent radio transmission static, but he knew his record was being checked.

After a few minutes, the officer pried himself out of his cruiser and returned to the curbside where Jupiter sat with his forearms on his knees and the fingers of his right hand clasped around his left thumb. Just then, Jupiter realized that the investigating officer was the same cop who sometimes moonlighted as a security guard at The Watercress, the luxury hotel where Jupiter worked as a dishwasher. Detail cops, as they were known, often took security jobs at private businesses to supplement their regular New Orleans Police Department salaries. This particular cop was on duty at The Watercress maybe once or twice a week, but with enough frequency that he felt right at home in the hotel's restaurant kitchen – comfortable enough to order club sandwiches and shrimp cocktails even when the employee meal for a particular day was some kind of cubed meat stew. This guy even had the nerve to eat his special meals right there in the kitchen in front of all the staff grunts who enjoyed no such privileges. Jupiter had to eat the regular offering even though he had invested a great deal of good will trying to curry favor with the cooks by regularly slipping bottled beer to them behind the hot line. Jupiter considered mentioning to the cop that they often worked at the same place, but rejected the idea as a sign of weakness. He didn't want the guy to think he needed to rely on special treatment.

"You need to get yourself a driver's license," said the officer. "What are you doing around here, anyway?"

"I live around here. I came to get a paperback to read on my streetcar ride to work. Is there a violation there somewhere?"

"Where's your mustache, Dawg?" asked the cop.

He wanted to say, "What need have I of a mustache in this feast of pure reason?" but the joke would have been completely lost on the plump corporal.

Instead he said, "Where is it? You mean, did I

misplace it?" Jupiter let the corner of his mouth rise into a sarcastic smile.

"What are you, a record player? Where's your flavor saver? I thought all you gangsters had mustaches."

"Um, I'm not sure what you mean, officer. Are you going to arrest me for *not* having a mustache?" Jupiter was beginning to have fun with the absurd colloquy. But the cop instantly turned hostile.

"Listen up," he said. "Are you on paper? You got anything on you I should know about? Any guns, knives, hand grenades, nuclear weapons?" The cop put his hands on Jupiter and lifted him up by his armpits. "Turn around," said the cop, as he searched Jupiter's mid-section and pockets. He placed his face as close as he could to Jupiter's right ear, as Jupiter was at least five inches taller than the swollen constable. The cop's breath smelled like boiled shrimp when he spoke:

"Is there some reason you don't have a mustache? Is it some kind of gang symbol? Are you a homo or something?" The cop spun Jupiter around by his shoulders so that they were as close as to face-to-face as they could be. In a gesture of utter disrespect, the cop put his fingers on Jupiter's face in what Jupiter knew was a demonstration of street superiority. Jupiter was able to stifle a natural reaction to this insult to his masculinity even though his heart began to thump in his chest. Jupiter caught sight of the cop's utility belt: nine millimeter automatic pistol, pepper spray, a Taser X26, and a telescoping police truncheon, all stowed snugly in their sure-fit safety holsters. Jupiter knew the cop was provoking him to resist the manhandling. But Jupiter stayed cool, in spite of the fact that the tips of the brass crescent on the policeman's chest badge were beginning to look like fangs.

"I don't have any weapons, or a mustache or a driver's license. I'm sorry to disappoint you but I don't have any of those things." Jupiter felt like he was getting himself on equal footing and the confrontation seemed to lose its volatility. Jupiter stood silently knowing it was the cop's turn to make a move.

"Why don't you get your paperback and be on your way." Jupiter had neutralized the cop's aggressiveness. But, before leaving, he scrutinized

Jupiter's face as if he had seen him before. Jupiter stared back but the cop made no immediate connection.

The cruiser slid away but Jupiter felt no sense of victory. To the contrary, he felt the strain of fascistic initiative. He felt his own insignificance and impotence. The entire episode was insulting, even infuriating. But it was typical, garden-variety racism that should not have threatened him, or so he hoped. Jupiter took a breath and decided to get his head right. He had to think about work, about Miss Josephine Boniface, his landlady, and about completing the simple mission of choosing a book to read. He also felt some satisfaction when reflecting on his new love interest: Gretchen Sobieski. Gretchen was a white girl from Pennsylvania he had met at his favorite bar in the Irish Channel. They had had a few dates and things looked promising. He didn't want to let overconfidence set him up for disappointment, so he directed his attention back to the Little Free Library.

The book he selected at last was *Carnival of Fury: Robert Charles and the New Orleans Race Riot of 1900* by William Ivy Hair. Jupiter knew vaguely of this incident from his research as an amateur student of New Orleans history. This book would provide him immediate amusement and make the streetcar ride to The Watercress tolerable. It was 8:00 AM, and he needed only to check on his landlady. He was leasing the one bedroom rental side of the double for $500 a month, which he paid promptly every month, and was a model tenant and model citizen. Jupiter owned few material possessions other than books and was generally able to keep his space tidy and clean in a responsible way that made his landlady, Josephine Boniface, happy. Jupiter's plan was to load his backpack, check on Miss Josephine and walk from his place on Monroe Street, down Oak Street to Carrollton Avenue where he would catch the streetcar and ride to The Watercress farther down the St. Charles Avenue line.

Josephine Boniface was the 76-year-old widow of Shadrach Boniface who had years earlier retired from his job as a maintenance man for New Orleans Public Service Incorporated, bought his home on Monroe Street in Pigeontown and then promptly died.

In that respect, Miss Josephine was a typical resident of the neighborhood, originally called "Pensiontown" after the many black pensioners who moved there after retiring. Jupiter figured the black inhabitants of the area must have mispronounced the name assigned by municipal bureaucrats and "Pigeontown" stuck.

The neighborhood was, of late, beginning to show signs of a demographic shift, the nascent stages of socio-racial residential displacement caused by rising real estate prices. The phenomenon, Jupiter knew, meant different things to different people, a resettlement that frequently occurred in older municipalities that have natural, confining barriers, like a river or a seashore. It was usually bad for poor folks who would be displaced by younger, white often cultivated adventurers seeking the richly textured experience of living among the authentic, the natives, the indigenous peoples of rugged asphalt. In time, housing costs would be naturally elevated until the original inhabitants could no longer afford to live there. At first, Jupiter felt that living in Pigeontown was a reflection of his appreciation for the old neighborhood and that he was demonstrating his beneficent commitment to community investment by indignantly keeping his residence there and helping Josephine Boniface maintain a secure and happy existence. But he did not want to be part of the displacement. He was, in a sense, torn.

Miss Josephine had stayed on in her Monroe Street home after her husband's death, proud to be a homeowner and content enough to collect monthly rent and Social Security. Miss Josephine was also a devoted member of True Light Baptist Church located only blocks away from the Monroe Street home. There were, in fact, no fewer than twelve neighborhood churches within walking distance that Jupiter could name, including Evening Star Missionary Baptist Church, Rising Star Missionary Baptist Church, Epiphany Evangelical Lutheran Church, Greater St. John the Baptist Church, Regular St. John the Baptist Church, New Haven Methodist Church, St. Joan of Arc Church (Catholic), St. Paul's African Methodist Episcopal Church, St. Mary's Church of God in Christ, Haven Trinity United Methodist Church and Prayer Tower

Church of God in Christ. Jupiter knew full well that all of these churches were tax dodges, ersatz charities that provided income to otherwise unemployed black ministers under the I.R.S. "parsonage exemption" and operating in a kind of parallel work force. Jupiter didn't care. Religion was for women and children anyway.

These churches were no bigger than the surrounding houses of the neighborhood and (with the exception of the Catholic church) held services for no more than 25 people at a time. They were all one-story, brick structures that stuck out among the worn Victorian and craftsman cottages of Pigeontown. Jupiter had noticed that many of these little churches were ornamented with midcentury modern decorative screen brick or patterned breeze block made popular in the 1940s and 50s by Edward Durell Stone, a Miesian apostate who had forsworn the International Style in favor of his own decorative idiosyncrasies and made famous by his design for the United States Embassy in New Delhi and the International Trade Mart building in New Orleans' central business district. How incongruous it was, Jupiter often pondered, that such an architectural style would find its way into Pigeontown and the tiny black Protestant churches of his neighborhood! But none of this really mattered to Jupiter Mingo on this hot September morning. He had to speak to Miss Josephine and he had to get to work at The Watercress.

Upon his arrival at the door of Miss Josephine's half of the Monroe Street double, he knocked lightly, called out her name and she appeared.

"Miss Josephine, I want you to start preparing to rent my apartment to a new tenant," said Jupiter with a touch of urgency. "I'm not going to be here forever, and you might as well take advantage of the Section 8 program so you can fetch a higher monthly rent," said Jupiter referring to the Federal Housing Authority program that provided rental assistance vouchers for the urban poor. As far as Jupiter could determine, the federal government began subsidizing urban housing in the 1930's to relieve the national embarrassment of destitute slum living at a time when rural laborers were migrating to cities like New Orleans where they could find work – primarily as longshoremen on the

Mississippi River docks. But by the 1970's, the program had created, it seemed to Jupiter, the reverse effect: poor people from the country with no employment prospects were flocking to urban areas to take advantage of the free housing. The federal government now had a massive housing obligation on its hands. The New Orleans economy simply could not absorb the resourceless populace. Jupiter felt the stress of this vacuum in Pigeontown where young black men his own age had nothing to do – the stultifying, intractable vagrancy of idle youth, recently graduated from high school in a job market unable to accommodate the great mass of unskilled laborers no longer the wards of the public school systems. Inevitably, neighborhood gangs sprouted up all over New Orleans. The black boys of Jupiter's Pigeontown neighborhood terrorized the older residents, carjacked disoriented Tulane students on weekend pub crawls and fought gun battles with rival gangs over crack cocaine distribution territory. The Pigeontown gang was known as "The Taliban," perpetually at war with the "Hot Glocks" and the "Mid-City Killers" whose turf was nearby. The Taliban had stolen more than one of Jupiter's smartphones at the point of a gun — the gangsters often disguised as construction workers in safety reflector vests that would dampen the suspicions of law-abiding neighborhood witnesses. But he never reported the robberies or assisted the police in apprehending the perpetrators. He was somehow sympathetic to the optionless lifestyle these boys pursued by default, an existence that offered nothing, apart from the criminal opportunity that idleness brings. Never mind that he didn't want to get shot for co-operating with the police. Retaliation killing to enforce witness silence was known as getting your "Issue," and quick retaliation was getting your "Issue like Patricia." Jupiter wanted no part of that street retribution. He couldn't possibly solve this problem before his shift started at The Watercress. He could, however use the federal housing program to help Miss Josephine.

Jupiter beseeched: "Instead of getting $500 a month from me, you could get $1400 from someone with a voucher."

"I don't want no Section 8 creatures up in my house pullin' the wires and floodin' the tub," she declared, exhibiting no sympathy for her fellow New Orleanians who just needed a place to live. "It just ain't worth it."

"All right, at least go out to the Lakefront Arena and submit your paperwork to qualify as a Section 8 landlord. If nothing else, you can at least have that as an option," explained Jupiter. "I filled out all the forms for you. All you need to do is go out to the arena and turn them in," said Jupiter, referring to the University of New Orleans Lakefront Arena where a housing fair was being held by the Housing Authority of New Orleans at UNO's Lake Pontchartrain campus. "Just call Mr. Rodney and he can ride you out there in his taxicab."

"I suppose I could," said Miss Josephine. "How long before you expect to move out?"

"No tellin'," said Jupiter. "Could be any day now, with things the way they are. I just want to make sure that you have a new tenant in place if I have to move on." Jupiter's plan, of course, was to figure out a way to move in with Gretchen Sobieski, but Miss Josephine didn't need to know that.

"Where you going to, anyway?" asked Miss Josephine.

"Nowhere in particular…It's just that, I don't like to stay in the same place too long. I get restless." In the back of his mind, Jupiter had designs on moving in with Gretchen, but another sense of urgency was at work. He had been preparing for some time to make a statement, to declare the significance of his existence, to demonstrate that he had a place in the world. Jupiter's capacity for toleration was very nearly filled. Every day, the forces of authority were becoming more and more oppressive: unwarranted law enforcement intrusion, deliberate mistreatment by his superiors at work motivated by personal insecurity and inadequacy on the part of men who seemed to take pleasure in exercising their nominal superiority, and now, the disapproval of the universe that he would presume to expect a romantic relationship with a white girl.

"You in some kind of trouble?" asked Miss Josephine.

"No, no, not at all. I just want to make sure you're all set if I get the wanderlust." Jupiter was not in any trouble at that moment, but he could not rule out that possibility in the future. His frustration with general circumstances was becoming intense. "Please, just go to the housing fair and fill out the forms. It will give me peace of mind." Jupiter felt a lump expand in his throat.

"I'll think about it," said Miss Josephine. "But it don't set too good with me."

Although he had, he hoped, convinced his landlady to go along with his plan, Jupiter began to have second thoughts. He was sending her into an extremely unsavory public assembly. Section 8 housing fairs were chaotic and depressing cattle calls – unwed, steatopygic, teen mothers in stretch pants and shower slippers, undisciplined children screaming and fighting, young tattooed black men in undershirts, long-haired, megaphone-wielding, white female organizers in ankle-strap, nylon sandals, row upon row of collapsible plastic chairs and air mattresses, picnic food, police monitors and an overall atmosphere of simmering violence. This would be no place for Miss Josephine. She was polite, unassuming and proper. The thought of her in her matching cornflower blue suit, pocketbook, stockings and alphabet-block heels amid this flotsam made him a little sick. *What have I done?*

The last, and only, time Jupiter had attended such an event was unforgettably unpleasant. Before he had moved in next to Miss Josephine, he had explored the possibility of obtaining a Section 8 voucher for himself, a humiliating exercise of last resort, but he could sure use the help. The local housing authority had announced that the number of available vouchers was being reduced for that year. Qualified applicants would only be awarded the remaining benefits on a first-come, first-served basis. Under those conditions, the horse race was going to fill very quickly. Jupiter rose early that day expecting to be at the front of the line at the former Flint-Goodrich Memorial Hospital on Louisiana Avenue, where a temporary voucher distribution tent had been set up.

But by the time Jupiter had arrived, the scene was already complete bedlam. Cars were parked on the neutral ground, police cruisers with flashing lights were blocking vehicular traffic on La Salle Street, black children were throwing beer cans at one another and middle-aged white men with earrings and underdeveloped calf muscles were trying to herd people into organized lines. Jupiter could not determine where exactly to begin his approach. There seemed to be some kind of official looking tent near the iron entrance gate to the old WPA-style hospital where the most noise was being made. He circled around a phalanx of parked SUV's that all had "Enterprise" rental decals on the bumpers. Their tailgates were down and some doors were open so that music could be offered to the slithering throngs of fair-goers. Jupiter came upon a young, fair-skinned black woman with a Jawbone cellular phone device attached to her right ear. She was wearing a T-shirt that read "Housing is a Right, Not a Privilege." Jupiter concluded that she would be helpful.

"Excuse me. Where does the application line form for Section 8 voucher applications?"

"You got to complete yo' pre-application form

'fo you get yo' application," she informed. Jupiter was about to inquire further about the process but she began speaking to an unseen person, apparently through her Jawbone microphone. Jupiter decided to continue his pursuit of rights and privileges on his own. He proceeded alongside the fence that enclosed the Flint-Goodrich building, now a low-income apartment complex for Section 8 seniors and small families. Jupiter looked up at the fine Depression-era, *Public Works Moderne* architectural style so often championed by out-of-work architects of the 1930's who benefited from the generous allowances of the Roosevelt administration. The building was truly beautiful and Jupiter congratulated himself for knowing that its shadow fell on the old Jewish neighborhood of Central City. He gripped two rungs of the iron fence with his hands and wiped his brow with the upper sleeve of his cotton shirt. *What am I doing at this housing fair madness? Get me outta here. Maybe I'll take a stroll to the scene of race riots of 1900. Take in Emile Weil's Anshe Sfard Synagogue over on Carondelet Street.* As the sun rose, Jupiter knew that he would forget about Section 8 vouchers and the agitated throngs bouncing about him.

"Do you like the building?" Someone was speaking to Jupiter over his left shoulder. He turned to see a bald-headed man with a beard and wire-rimmed glasses wearing a light-blue, oxford-cloth, buttoned down shirt and un-pleated khaki dungarees. "The Flint-Goodrich building. Quite a nice building, don't you think?"

Jupiter looked at the middle-aged white man and said, "Oh yes, quite nice. Lots of these people would like to live there, I'm sure." Jupiter wanted to be polite and, at the same time, inject some socially conscious concern for the people swarming about them.

"My grandfather, Moise Goldstein, designed it in 1932 for Dillard University," said the gentleman who seemed keen to express his solidarity with Jupiter's blackness. But he wasn't trying *too* hard. He was being friendly, but not patronizing. Jupiter didn't want to be too sensitive about these kinds of encounters with eager Jewish liberals. He could certainly be affable in return.

"Is that right," said Jupiter. "I've always admired this building. Your grandfather designed many fine buildings in New Orleans. Are you an architect as well?"

"As a matter of fact I am. I moved to New York after graduation, but I love coming home. Especially since the Katrina levee failures. There's so much to be done in bringing back the housing stock."

Jupiter recognized all the code words the man was using. "Levee failure" meant that the federal government was grossly negligent and depleted "housing stock" meant that black neighborhoods had been washed away by an insensitive bureaucratic Leviathan. Jupiter didn't want to give the impression that he was willing to join hands in an exalted political cause, but he still didn't want to seem cold.

"Yes, well, I was checking out the housing fair myself. But, as you can see, everything is *tohu bohu*, as they say." Jupiter chuckled nervously to soften the Hebrew reference.

"Ah, yes, very good! *Tohu bohu* indeed!" replied the friendly pilgrim. Jupiter smelled Yale.

"Do you work for the City?"

"Oh, no!" said Jupiter, expressing a humorous disavowal of any organization associated with the three-ring circus being staged around them. "I work at The Watercress."

"The Watercress!" the man exclaimed. "Designed by Weiss, Dreyfous. My brother-in-law owns the place! Maybe you know him? His name's Shale Gimmelfarb?"

Jupiter thought he recognized the name, but he knew he had never met the owner. "No, I've never met him. Is he a local?"

"Oh yes. Actually his name is Shale Gimmel. I don't know why I keep saying Gimmel*farb*. I guess that was his name in the Old Country. Anyway, he's married to my sister. I'm sure you'll run across him soon enough. He's always there fussing over the property. Tell him we spoke. I'm sure he'd like to meet you."

Jupiter was sure the owner of The Watercress would not be interested in meeting one of his dishwashers. Unless, of course, he wanted to pad his statistics on "Black People With Whom I am Acquainted." On second thought, Jupiter might be able to use that to his advantage.

"Anyway, I've got to get going," said Jupiter. "Welcome back. I hope you stay a while and enjoy your time in your home town," said Jupiter, fearing that the man would discover that he was actually here to apply for his own Section 8 voucher.

"Yes I will," said the man. "So long, and best of luck my friend."

Jupiter turned and tried to dissolve into the crowd. The encounter was somewhat unsettling and he sensed an urgent need to escape from the oppressive assembly of ill-clad urban homesteaders. No more housing fairs for Jupiter.

That memory haunted Jupiter as he considered sending his landlady, Miss Josephine, out to the UNO Lakefront Arena for what would be a similar experience. Jupiter could imagine her reaction: "I got no business mixin' with that crowd." Still, getting her established as a qualified Section 8 landlord was critical to her future in Pigeontown should Jupiter have to relocate on short notice. Jupiter felt guilty for putting her through the ordeal, especially when his motives were so selfish. But thoughts of Gretchen seemed to come before anything else.

Jupiter boarded the streetcar and sat next to his backpack for the thirty-minute ride to The Watercress and slouched into a tarnished wooden bench seat on the starboard side.

Work at The Watercress began every day at 10 AM and it sucked. His boss was Brandon Cazenave, a thirty year-old, light-skinned black Catholic who, like most Creoles of color in New Orleans, looked down on dark-skinned blacks like Jupiter blaming them for stunting their social ascendance and tainting public perception of them generally. Jupiter resented Brandon Cazenave's attitude and the Creole condescension that had been a part of intramural black relations since New Orleans was founded. Jupiter knew that Brandon knew he lived in Pigeontown and that he considered it a place where lower-class blacks resided. Brandon and the Cazenave family lived in Voscoville, a neighborhood near Elysian Fields in the Seventh Ward where an enclave of light-skinned, mixed-race New Orleanians was able to isolate itself. They attended Corpus Christi Catholic Church and carried on their lives as a segregated sub-group. This neighborhood produced those well-to-do, freckle-faced mulatto politicians, mostly female of late, who, with the sentimental votes of race-conscious whites, served on the city council, utility commissions, domestic courts and what was left, after Hurricane Katrina, of the Orleans Parish School Board. These female politicos always hyphenated their last names, which irritated Jupiter. In the 1980's and 90's they started retaining their birth names after marriage to take advantage of any familiarity black voters might have with their activist fathers from historically established political families from the civil rights era. Eventually, these light-skinned Creole women adopted the practice of hyphenation to separate themselves from the unwed Baby Mamas from the projects whom they secretly scorned. Jupiter hated them for this haughtiness. More than that, Jupiter despaired at the prospect of an already maternally-based *domestic* black underclass becoming maternally-based on the *political* level as well. Even more recently, a coterie of Creole lesbians had emerged as electable politicians and further established the matriarchal domination of the black community. Black men like Jupiter had been reduced to a demographic statistic.

In his curiosity, Jupiter Mingo had conducted some field research on this "Voscoville" neighborhood: according to residents he had importuned, "Voscoville" was really a sanitized rechristening of "Boscoville," a colloquial name taken from the Bosco chocolate syrup that turned milk light brown. The connotation of the nickname was that the residents were a mixture of black and white blood, just like chocolate milk. Mud Ducks with a light brown skin color and an attitude of superiority over pure blacks. Although Jupiter could never really get a straight answer, he concluded that the nickname "Boscoville" existed for decades until the neighborhood improvement association decided to assume a less race-based title. Boscoville's reputation for hostility toward dark-skinned blacks like Jupiter was legendary and continued to be a source of embarrassment to the precinct's leaders who were forever taking pains to suppress any cultural evidence that one sub-group of blacks harbored any openly racist attitudes towards another. So the neighborhood's contemporary residents would flatly deny that the name "Boscoville" ever existed. If the story the residents told was to be believed, and light-skinned Creoles looked down upon pure Africans like Jupiter, his resentment towards Brandon Cazenave and his ilk had a rational basis.

But Jupiter was always very careful with this information. The resentment dark-skinned blacks harbored against their mixed-race relatives was positively *not* for white consumption. Black political power depended on some measure of solidarity. Yet Jupiter knew that the hostility sometimes bubbled up to the surface. He had discovered that, in the earliest stages of the civil rights movement, around 1938, a light-skinned black man named Walter F. White visited New Orleans to deliver a speech in his capacity as Executive Secretary of the National Association for the Advancement of Colored People. Halfway through his remarks, he dropped a bombshell: "Negroes and

Creoles maintain a division in New Orleans that is a definite hindrance to their progress." Local Creoles, many of them members of the Aristocrat Club that had been formed to separate themselves socially from the dark multitudes, were outraged and several local leaders publicly responded that an attitude of "mutual cooperation" and "bosom friendship" prevailed. Jupiter concluded that White had stumbled upon an historic animosity between "Uptown blacks" and "Downtown Creoles" and decided to openly declare that the more privileged of the two groups was guilty of exclusionary policies and economic relegation. The leadership of the more socially prominent and politically active Creole community, which was at that time led by men, reacted sharply and defensively to an "age-old assumption" that should be "discarded for mutual cooperation." To them, White was an unwitting agitator and he very nearly cracked open a fault line that would compromise the political effectiveness of the Black-Creole bloc vote. Open hostilities were quickly stuffed under the cushions, so to speak, but the mutual resentment lingered. Everyone in black and semi-black New

Orleans knew the unspoken reality. Jupiter's discovery of this controversy confirmed what he already knew from experience. His boss, Brandon Cazenave, exhibited it every day. But it was a state of affairs that must be hidden as much as possible. He would never disclose such a sensitive issue, not Jupiter, to a white community that might use it for political mischief.

Lately it seemed, though wherefore he knew not, the world Jupiter inhabited had become a sterile promontory: A world he perceived abstractly as one of colorful circles gently bouncing against one and other in an incidental pageant, a bustling but never bursting congregation of spectral bubbles. Yet more and more, especially in times of ordinary stress, the mental images had become more angular. Faces and forms assumed menacing, hostile impressions that set his teeth on edge. Bitter droplets of black bile seemed on those occasions to drip from his nasal cavity onto the back of his tongue and literally put a bad taste in his mouth despoiling his usually measured demeanor of equanimity. What a piece of work he was this Jupiter Mingo! *Mandingo Furioso!* He would have to watch this development very closely.

Jupiter had been claiming to be descended from a notorious revolutionary slave. But that was not his only biographical fabrication. Years before, he had carefully embroidered a *resumé* designed to impress public school administrators who were hiring high school English teachers. His plan worked, the administrators were fooled and he was hired to teach literature classes to teenagers enrolled in Central City's E. Arnold Bertonneau High School. Jupiter was willing to overlook the fact that the school's namesake was a free man of color of French-Catholic descent – the very ethnic group that continued to look down on men like Jupiter in contemporary New Orleans. Jupiter lasted only half a semester at Bertonneau High before the light-skinned, French-Catholic administrators (all of them women) and the absentee California white man who had been awarded the charter school contract to run Bertonneau High uncovered the ruse. They immediately terminated Jupiter's employment contract. Jupiter would have been humiliated had not the administrators and owner treated him with such condescension.

Standing in ignominious abjection upon the blasted asphalt where his school stood, Jupiter was irritated and left with a sense of emptiness. As he exited the backdoor of Bertonneau High for the last time, he was approached by a black janitor named Cleveland Peete who attempted to comfort him. Cleveland's kind words suggested that he empathized with Jupiter's circumstances and confirmed Jupiter's suspicions that dark-skinned blacks constituted the lowest hash mark of the social yardstick that seemed to measure a wide range of pigmented New Orleanians. It was the first instance Jupiter could remember perceiving his surroundings in angular shapes through a darkened scrim. The faces of the school administrators had lost their roundness and took on the sinister tenacity of Medieval beasts, like creatures in a Hieronymous Bosch painting or the Apocalypse Tapestries of Angiers. Drip, drip, drip. The black bile deposited its bitterness on the back of Jupiter's throat. All the world crumpled itself up into angles and spurs and spears and spikes and pikes and falchions and poignards and corseques and sparths and flechettes! Where had all the flowers gone? The soft pillows? The pastel balloons? The bosom of Abraham?

At the very moment of that hallucination, Cleveland handed Jupiter a heavy nylon athletic bag emblazoned with the Bertonneau High logo. Only later did Jupiter peer into the bag to determine its contents: a very compact and futuristically designed assault weapon of some sort, the likes of which Jupiter had never seen.

"What's this?" asked Jupiter.

"You never know," said Cleveland. "You might need it."

"Looks like you could do some serious damage with this thing," said Jupiter, as he surveyed the weapon's oddly ergonomic angularity. "You never know when things might get serious." Jupiter knew what he meant but just what purpose he might put to the implement he could not say. That much was soon to become clear.

As he pondered that brief colloquy with Cleveland, things began to seem organized in his head, save for one little personal matter. A matter that was, perhaps, more important than all others: Gretchen Sobieski. They had met in one of the dozen or so Irish Channel saloons so common in that old, riverside neighborhood. Gretchen had sought him out at the corner of the bar where they spent the next three hours talking. She worked for a non-profit organization promoting environmental consciousness and even had a tattoo on her right shoulder. It was the universal recycling logo — three green and yellow bent vector arrows circling clockwise. She had a slim, athletic *(breasts like 1952 chrome Chrysler bumper guards!)*, and wavy brown hair. And she was white. *Mandigo Innamorato!* Just as he began to wonder whether that mattered, Jupiter's smartphone rang. It was Gretchen. But the call did not come through.

The failed call triggered another moment of insecure self-reflection. Jupiter's own personal heritage was unknown to him, as his parents died when he was very young. So he made one up. His last name, Mingo, he would thenceforth explain, came from one of the leaders of the Andry Plantation slave uprising in the early 1800s. One of the organizers of the rebellion was named simply "Mingo" and Jupiter told everybody that he could trace his lineage directly back to him. The revolt was quickly put down by a local militia. Mingo was lynched and had his severed head put on a pole as a warning to other slaves, but not before he was able to procreate and begin a line of descendents that led directly to Jupiter. In this way, Jupiter Mingo found his place in the world.

This moment of reflection became a moment of confused reverie as he gazed from the window of the streetcar at the mansions pitched in the mud along St. Charles Avenue. *L'habitant de la cabane et celui du palais, tout souffre, tout gémit ici-bas.* Jupiter reflected upon the racial dividing line that St. Charles Avenue had become Post-Katrina, or, really, what it had always been once bedroom communities sprouted upriver, one after another, beginning in the mid-1800's as New Orleans expanded in that direction. Jupiter figured that the more expensive real estate must have been closest to the railway that would become the St. Charles Avenue streetcar line stretching all the way from the

Old Quarter to what would become his Pigeontown neighborhood and beyond. Blacks never ventured across St. Charles Avenue from their Central City enclave unless they wanted to be confronted by private security patrols: racial profiling in Cisalpine Gaul, as Jupiter referred to the all-white Garden District that was situated on one side of the streetcar line. The other, all-black side, which nobody ever ventured or bothered to chart, he referred to as Transalpine Gaul. The unknown land. But it wasn't unknown to Jupiter. He had walked the length and breadth of the district looking for the ghost of Robert Charles (the turn-of-the-century, Black Revolutionary subject of the biography he had found earlier that day), but very few had risked a stroll through the Garden District to be subjected to the private security patrols hired by nervous whites with disposable after-tax dollars. But Jupiter's selfish indulgence to begrudge whites their material possessions was interrupted by thoughts of his new book. *Carnival of Fury: The Robert Charles riot of 1900* was named for a Columbus, Mississippi, laborer who moved to New Orleans and rented an apartment near where The Watercress now stood. According to the book, Charles took up a variety of jobs, but never married. While in New Orleans, he sold newspapers and became involved in a back-to-Africa movement based in Atlanta. Charles had befriended a Jewish clothing salesman named Hyman Levy and began to frequent the Dryades Street neighborhood where Eastern European Jews had established a retail merchant market place, also only blocks from The Watercress. One evening in 1900, police were summoned to investigate two Negro hoodlums who were loitering near the house of a white woman. One of the miscreants turned out to be Robert Charles, and when the police tried to arrest him, Charles fired at them and fled. Jupiter imagined that Robert Charles knew the drip, drip, drip of black bile and the angular mutation that humanity could present.

Eventually, as the account held, a mustered police contingent cornered Charles at the annex of a friend's Saratoga Street home. During the standoff, Charles killed or wounded several police officers, including a captain of the command. Charles was able to fight off the assault for hours armed with a rifle (used in an earlier altercation in Mississippi) and homemade bullets he fashioned by melting sections of lead pipe. Although Charles himself was eventually killed, riotous skirmishes continued around town until order was restored a few weeks later. The author's recitation of typically spurious folklore held that Charles was celebrated as a hero by the black community for a short time. In fact, Jupiter remembered that the great jazz pioneer and fabulist "Jelly Roll" Morton spoke about the Robert Charles incident in his interview with Alan Lomax, a folk historian and crypto-communist who toured the country chronicling regional music forms. At the time of the interview in the 1940's, Jelly Roll was still uncomfortable discussing the matter. Jelly Roll said he remembered occasionally playing a rag-time tune written about the tragedy, complete with hagiographic lyrics. Jelly Roll thought it best to forget that tune and claimed he never played it again. Jupiter was suspicious of Jelly Roll and concluded there never was such a song and that he was making up a story Lomax might find authentic and recordable, something with anecdotal texture. Jupiter was not interested in texture.

In time, the story of Robert Charles, and the racial injustices to which he was subject, faded from memory. But it began to resonate in Jupiter Mingo as he read from his new book. He concluded that Robert Charles was an innocent man, wrongfully harassed by racist and superstitious Irish and Italian police goons. That kind of harassment was very familiar to Jupiter. He had smelled the fetid breath of the New Orleans Police Department earlier that very day. Just before he exited the streetcar for work, Jupiter Mingo felt his hatred for the white man, on top of his hatred for the almost white man, begin to boil.

On the short walk between the streetcar stop at the corner of Jackson Avenue and the employee entrance of The Watercress on Josephine Street, Jupiter stopped and took an inventory of his backpack. The contents were:

His newly-acquired copy of *Carnival of Fury: Robert Charles and the New Orleans Race Riot of 1900*

A Latin-English dictionary

The transcript of the complete Alan Lomax interviews of Jelly Roll Morton

A book entitled *Social Control in Slave Plantation Societies* by Gwendolyn Midlo Hall (a racial progressive and FBI subversive who married a communist black man in the 1940s)

Another book entitled *Time's Tapestry: Four Generations of a New Orleans Family* by Leta Weiss Marks (daughter of Leon Weiss of the architectural firm Weiss, Dreyfous)

A bottle of water

A cigarette lighter

His smartphone

And, finally, a Belgian Fabrique Nationale Herstal P90 5.7 mm Bullpulp submachine gun with straight blowback, closed-bolt action and two fifty-round detachable box magazines

Jupiter was ready for work

Chapter 3
Pyramid Schemes

AT 8 O'CLOCK ON THE MORNING OF Jupiter Mingo's streetcar ride to work at The Watercress, 32-year-old Maunsel (pronounced "MAN-suhl") Williams Blackshear descended the staircase of his swell uptown home on Coliseum Street in the Hurstville section of Uptown New Orleans. His toilet complete and his business casual uniform fitted sharply around his slim frame, he was ready to greet his 28-year-old wife, Haydée ("EYE-DAY"), and their one-year-old daughter, Mathilde ("MAH-TEEL"), before heading out to his job as an annuity salesman at his office downtown on Poydras Street. He was an Episcopalian, of the well-flannelled Brahman sort, but he had married a Catholic girl to the deflation of his anti-Papist, room-temperature parents. His mother, like many American Episcopalian women, was anti-Catholic, mostly because she found them displeasing to be around in a, well, *ethnic*, fishmonger, body odor kind of a way. In New Orleans, it was difficult for Episcopalians like Maunsel's mother to express their dislike of Catholics who, after all, occupied an elevated social position inherited from the original French oligarchs of the colonial period. Unable to condescend openly to Catholics as was customary in New England and among the Knickerbocker elite in places like Suffolk County, Episcopalians in New Orleans like Maunsel's mother simply joined Planned Parenthood. They had no interest in the biological equivalency Planned Parenthood championed for women, nor did they give any thought to the Constitutional penumbrae vouchsafed by the United States Supreme Court. Being anti-abortion was a way for Episcopalians to segregate themselves from Catholics on the opposite side of a very bright line. When pressed for an explanation about her support for Planned Parenthood, Maunsel's mother would never divulge the fact she was only using the organization as a mechanism to broadcast her anti-Catholic prejudice. That animus was never to be openly divulged, so she manufactured distracting pretexts to avoid any serious discussions on the topic. Very often, Maunsel's mother would slyly intimate a racial basis for her casual support for abortion so as to neutralize any speculation that she had anything in mind other than to prevent *blacks* from procreating. "Well, we've got to do *something* about babies having babies in the housing projects," she would say. Any discussion of abortion rights would then come to a screeching halt because no one, at least no one in white Uptown society, would challenge the notion that black reproduction needed to be curtailed. An appeal to anti-black prejudices would always divert any suspicion that Episcopalians were anti-Catholic and camouflage the real reason behind what would ordinarily be a very controversial political position in favor of abortion – as if to say, "We Episcopalians favor abortion because we don't like blacks*, not* because we don't like Catholics." But deep-seated anti-Catholicism was the atavistic impulse that preoccupied Maunsel's mother and her similarly situated Episcopalian broodmares. That prejudice, which was formidable in Maunsel's parents' generation, and still evident in his, had not diminished his attraction to Haydée's sorority-girl pulchritude.

Society Catholic girls in New Orleans, as opposed to Irish or Italian or Croatian ones who lived in Metairie or Kenner or Chalmette, all had gallophile names with lots of vowels like Haydée, Mathilde, Renée ("Ruh-NAY"), Aimée (A-MAY"), Amélie ("AH-muh-lee") or Mignon ("MEE-yon"). Maunsel was used to it, and he was willing to honor, up to a point, the unspoken rule of Episcopalian society that discouraged Anglican intermarriage with the Catholic *sans culottes*. After all, the Cabots spoke only to the Blackshears, and the Blackshears spoke only to God. But when Haydée and her sorority sisters from Queen's College, North Carolina, made a road trip to the University of Virginia in Charlottesville when Maunsel was a senior, he was thunderstruck. Eight years later, they were married at Holy Name of Jesus Catholic Church on St. Charles Avenue with a reception following at the New Orleans Country Club in strict accordance with the accepted society protocol. Baby Mathilde arrived two years later.

As Maunsel breezed into his Viking/SubZero kitchen equipped with drawers that glided closed without slamming when you pushed them in, Baby Mathilde was in her high chair fingering Cheerios cereal ringlets and scattering them across her plastic baby tray before placing them daintily into her little mouth, blissfully oblivious to her morganatic pedigree. Haydée seemed to be hard at work with paper and pen scribbling like a customs clerk on a raised chair pushed to the edge of the kitchen island and holding her shoulder length blonde hair away from her delicate face in deep concentration. He expected to see his wife wearing her juice-box mommy daytime weekday wardrobe: J Brand, mid-rise, skinny or boot-cut white jeans in one of the available and various stages of factory-simulated deterioration (distressed, demented, dissolute, destroyed) with a jewel-toned, single pocket silk blouse by Equipment and Corky's cork platform wedge heels with crisscrossed natural leather top straps and ankle buckles. Instead, she was wearing her workout gear: Lulu Lemon runner-skirt (he recognized it from the upside down horseshoe logo), a racerback tank in hot pink and a Soju light blue running bra (showing). Her shoes were neon green, fuchsia and chartreuse Brooks brand minimal running shoe with no-show anklet socks. She wore a yellow Fitbit heart-rate monitoring device on her left wrist. He remembered she had purchased this get-up at one of her friend's private-home, husband-sponsored trunk shows, the profits of which were no doubt eaten up by the catering costs for goat cheese crostinis with fig compote, ham and Gruyere thumbprints, Caprese salad skewers with bird's eye pepper balsamic drizzle, sparkling cranberry Brie bites, blistered counterfeit glance beets and double elephant sheet pastry chouquettes.

"Whatcha working on, Sweetie?" inquired Maunsel, not the slightest little bit interested in any response. Baby Mathilde chirped and squeaked happily as Cheerios fell to the floor.

"I'm in charge of the invitations for this year's

ArtUbator Fundraiser," she replied without looking up. "The title I've come up with is 'Starry Starry Night' and the theme is French Impressionism. Ya know, like what we saw at the Musée d'Orsay 'cuz its like a museum fundraiser." After three years of marriage, Maunsel had come to realize that Haydée was not drawing from a teeming portfolio of clever aphorisms. He braced for her recital of the invitation copy she was composing. He couldn't help but recall the doggerel she had written for a Mexican-themed 30th birthday surprise party for her sister, Thérèse ("Tuh-REZ"). He knew it by heart:

Don't just lay there and siesta, it's time to fiesta!

January 14 is the date, so don't be late!

The time is 7:30, so wear something flirty.

Señores y Senoritas, come enjoy margaritas!

Thérèse has a birthday. Olé! Guacamole!

Wear your poncho or serape, it'll be 100% agave!

Keep it under your sombrero (it's a surprise!)

5422 Coliseum St.

No presents, por favor

RSVP Haydée (hblackshear@gmail.com)

By the time she had crafted that gem, Maunsel had abandoned any desire to help Haydée with her occasional projects and had resorted to fake smiles and insincere encouragement. He would say, "Hey, that sounds great!" or "Wow! You've done it again!" In their goofier courtship days, he would gently correct her when she said "mis-CHEE-vee-ous," "per-RIF-fee-al" and "vin-uh-ger-ETTE" and "REE-luh-ter." She was the Carol Brady of dyslexic epenthesis. But he no longer cared. She was a beautiful girl who took care of their beautiful child and never complained that they never had sex anymore. Maintaining a cynicism-free environment at home was essential for the smooth operation of his extra-marital dalliances. He had more important things on his mind, such as fucking his new girlfriend, Kirstin Duplechain, a paralegal he met months earlier at a Tarpon Bar happy hour. Kirsten was no Dorothy Parker herself but she had a meretricious allure that got his motor running. When you have a girlfriend like that on the side, and men in his position were *supposed* to have girlfriends on the side, you had to make everything at home flow as seamlessly as possible. This included, of course, enthusiastic support for the wife's stay-at-home pastimes. On this particular September morning, Maunsel prepared himself for Haydée's description of the party invitation she was designing for some kind of art museum fundraiser.

Maunsel would come to find out that a nonprofit arts promotion organization, nominally funded by City Hall, was raising money to benefit an ambitious program called "ArtUbator" (as in, "Arts Incubator") slated to occupy the building at the corner of Howard and Carondelet Streets. The building previously housed the since defunct "Louisiana ArtWorks" project, the ambitious brainchild of the Arts Council of New Orleans. Millions upon millions of dollars had been spent to renovate the old Bradford Furniture Warehouse, an Arts and Crafts masterpiece designed by Leon Weiss (later of Weiss, Dreyfous). The building was erected in 1915 but had been covered with gold aluminum cladding in the 1960s and then altogether abandoned in the 1980s. The City of New

Orleans acquired the place in the mid-2000s and donated it to the Arts Council to do with as it saw fit. Upon receipt of huge budget outlays from the Louisiana state legislature, the Arts Council formed "Louisiana ArtWorks" to promote and outfit the facility as a work space for people Maunsel never knew or even saw: artists, artisans and craftsmen (painters, sculptors, glass-blowers, metalworkers, tanners, bead stringers, candle makers, pottery throwers, and so forth). Huge amounts of money had been spent to install blast furnaces, sheet metal presses, plaster mixing machines, leather tanning vats, pneumatic power-tool motors, acid bath tubs, industrial ventilation, jumbo laser printers, electric pottery wheels and the like. Other parts of the building were set aside for artist lofts and work stalls for the expected throngs of starving art visionaries who could not otherwise afford their own studios to craft their various and invaluable contributions to what Maunsel had always been told was elevated culture. At the grand opening, when the facility was made available to them for use, nobody showed up. Within a year, the whole boondoggle folded and the renovated building languished as a security and insurance albatross for the City and a budgeting headache for the City Council's general fund.

To the rescue came the Tikkun Olam Foundation of Boca Raton and its $2 million bequest to the Arts Council for the ArtUbator project. The donation was contingent upon the collection of matching funds from the City's "Percent for Art" program and private donations. Haydée was not the chairman (chairperson/chairwoman/chair) of the charity, but she had by that time moved steadily up the quasi-society pyramid to become Party Theme and Invitation Coordinator. Maunsel had long-since concluded that these charity organizations in New Orleans, attempting to emulate similar ones in New York, were essentially pyramid schemes. Bored, juice-box housewives would start out in the enlisted infantry, attending organizational meetings, hitting the streets to secure in-kind donations from local merchants, manning the phone banks to solicit cash contributions and generally serving as footsoldier functionaries for whatever needed to be done. Over time, girls like Haydée would eventually achieve more authoritative positions such as subcommittee chair, industry liaison, or food and beverage coordinator. Ultimately, if she genuflected properly and offered up the requisite flattery to that year's leadership and members of the Arts Council Board, she would become Chair of the following year's overall program. The process would continue year after year so long as lower-level aspirants from the new-mommy ranks could be drawn into the scheme. For that, these charitable organizations would carefully — Maunsel was tempted to say "spitefully" — cultivate the untapped envy and social aspiration of other wealthy, married, white women. Haydée was well-away in her ascent to the top of the Arts Council pyramid.

Haydée, Maunsel knew, was keenly aware of this dynamic, though it would never have occurred to her to characterize it as an organized or systematic process. Maunsel knew it oh-too-well, for he was involved in his own society pyramid scheme at his downtown men's lunch club, The Lancaster Club.

These organizations, the aristocratic institutions of New Orleans male, white society for over 100 years, mapped out their internal hierarchies in exactly the same way that charity fundraising organizations did for their wives. First of all (and here they were starkly different from the money-driven charity circuit) they were rigidly exclusive – no blacks, no Loyola Dagoes, no Choctaw Club Irish Old Regulars (New Orleans' version of Tammany Hall from 1900 to 1940, once known as "The Ring"), no random, newly-rich tycoons of any stripe (car dealership emperors, oil field service industry czars, fast food kings, funeral service industrialists, cheese-ball trial lawyer Guidos, *etc.*) and, since the early 20th century, no Jews. Incongruously, certain westernized, aristocratic, German Jews from the earlier migration were, at the turn of the 20th century, invited to join such clubs on the condition that they displayed sufficient cultural assimilation. But those few lucky ones — beautiful, elegant gentlemen like Judah Benjamin, Samuel Delgado, Benjamin Jonas, Charles Seixas, Adolph Meyer and Julius Weis — were quietly squeezed out of the men's clubs when, in the 1920s and 30s, the Orthodox Ashkenazim began to flood the streets with their funny hats and stinky food. Maunsel often wondered whether those older, completely westernized Jewish families resented the Eastern European newcomers for their obnoxious intrusion. Apart from that incidental reflection, Maunsel didn't really care.

With or without Jewish membership, the Lancaster Club pyramid scheme worked in a way that would be familiar to Haydée and her fellow charity fundraiser operatives. You began by coveting an invitation to join one or more of the men's lunch clubs. Upon admission, if you were lucky, you attended lunch every weekday, fucked off in the card room, engaged in whimsical, beneficent yet condescending banter with the black staff on a first name basis as much as possible, and then jockeyed for one of the lower level administrative positions that came with a coveted title. Soon enough, you might be appointed some kind of sergeant-at-arms, wild game-dinner coordinator, third vice-president or kitchen liaison. Through the years, you would rise to the position of Secretary or Treasurer in hopeful expectation that you would one day assume the post of President of the club or, better still, king of the affiliated carnival ball. But, as with any pyramid scheme, this upward thrust required the influx of new covetousness and social ambition from the emerging white boy professionals. Post-Katrina, the pyramid scheme was showing no signs of collapse.

All of this flashed through Maunsel's mind in an instant, aware of it, as he was, on a sub-cellular level. There was no point pondering the merits of the whole thing, let alone his personal position within it. The task at hand was to serve as a sounding board for his wife's entertainment vision: the Impressionism-themed party invitation for ArtUbator.

"The invitation is going to be tri-fold and the cover will be an impressionistic picture of the Bradford Furniture Warehouse against van Gogh's 'Starry Night' skyscape," allowed Haydée. Maunsel sipped his coffee and made googly eyes at Baby Mathilde. "As you open the invitation, the left side will list the schedule of party-night events – patron party at seven, *hors d'oeuvres* and champagne at seven-thirty, dancing and silent auction at eight, *etc.*," she explained. "The center interior panel will have a short bio of The Tikkun Olam foundation of Boca Raton followed by a list of corporate sponsors and private foundation donors."

"Tikkun Olam?" asked Maunsel. "What's that?"

"It's the group that pledged the $2 million seed money for the ArtUbator project. I'm going to put a brief summary of its institutional mission on the center panel:

> The mission of TOFBR is to cultivate diversity and promote the participation and mentoring of minorities, women and members of the LGBT community in the arts and arts-related pursuits in urban areas where they have been traditionally underserved.

"LGBT?" asked Maunsel. "What's that?"

"Lesbian, gay, bisexual and transgendered," said Haydée, proud to reel off this bit of cutting edge, pop culture ephemera.

Maunsel thought to himself, "What about hermaphrodites? Hermaphrodites are people, too, aren't they? And don't forget eunuchs." But he decided, judiciously (*phew!*), to suppress that bit of sarcasm. It was no time for sarcasm. He had fucking his mistress on his mind and only supportive enthusiasm for his wife's project was called for. "Well, that sounds like a worthwhile endeavor." *No point interrupting this interminable presentation.*

"On the third interior panel will be a list of private individual donors ranked by amount pledged. $5000 will be the Magnificent Monets. $2500 will be the Vivacious van Goghs. $2000, the Dynamic Degas. $1000, the Radiant Renoirs and $500 and below the eLectric Lautrecs."

"How very clever, Honey," Maunsel chimed. "Sounds like the invitation is really coming together!" Wow, he pondered. Magnificent Monets. People would actually be reading these lists — people in his socio-economic stratum who were watching his (and his wife's) movements, his situation, and (most important) his level of material consumption very closely.

Maunsel was watching them, too.

And it all began with the house on Coliseum Street. He paid $825,000 for the three bedroom/three bath renovated Victorian in the no-flood section of Uptown on the river side of St. Charles Avenue and the downtown side of Audubon Park – the perfect-prime location within striking distance of all the right schools, restaurants and daytime boutiques, and within blocks of all the young professionals and their wives who would be monitoring each other and keeping score. An $80,000 down payment meant his monthly mortgage note came to approximately $5000. His wife had to have a luxury SUV (festooned with all the requisite tailgate stickers representing school affiliation, private security district, anodyne preservation causes, country club memberships, *etc.*). He, personally, drove a $62,000 BMW sedan (7 series, because anything lower meant he was a junior player). Another $12,000 a year for Baby Mathilde's "Too Precious! Playpatch" nursery school tuition (twice a week for 45 minutes a day from September to May). And then there was "vay-kay" as his wife called it: $8000 a year for one trip to a

Caribbean island (a must) and $6000 for two trips a year to Grayton Beach, Florida, in a 17 bedroom air conditioned, balsa wood play house shared with two other image-conscious families. His wife referred to this as her "Happy Place," a term of art among juice-box mommies that irritated Maunsel for its delighted hackney, particularly because his "Happy Place" was eating pimento cheese sandwiches while watching pornographic movies on his personal computer. There were Junior League membership dues for Haydée and Lancaster Club dues for him. Carnival parade memberships (three) plus costs for parade throws (beads, doubloons, cups, stuffed animals, rubber spears, trinkets, *etc*.). Carnival parade membership for Haydée (plus parade throws). Country club dues, tennis club dues, private security detail subscriptions, insurance for everything, dinners at Robespierre, Maringouin's, The Ramekin and all the new Magazine Street bistros. His share of the $3000 fishing camp and 26-foot fishing boat with twin Yamaha 300 horsepower outboard motors. Not to mention utilities, groceries and baby things, plus the money Haydée spent as an idle housewife with nothing to do when he was away at work. With his $300,000 a year salary, he was not keeping the water from coming over the transom.

Maunsel had tried to think of ways to make money faster than by selling annuities. *If only I had a family business!* He even considered madcap lifelines like the reverse mortgages advertised on late-night television with aging sitcom stars as spokesmen. Lately, he had even taken to purchasing Powerball lottery tickets when the nationwide jackpots surpassed $100 million.

And still, on this particular morning, Maunsel had to get to the office and start making money the only way he could: selling annuities to injured plaintiffs recently flush with court settlements, Vietnamese restaurant owners with huge cash reserves stuffed under their floor boards, and friends of his parents. For that, he had to get to his office.

"Okay, Baby, I've got to get to work."

"Oh, Honey, don't forget," said Haydée as he headed for the door, "we need Brass Pass VIP tickets to this year's Jazz Fest. 'Train Smoke' Henry

Hitchcock is playing this year and my buds from Memphis are coming down to see him."

" 'Train Smoke' Henry what?"

"Hitchcock. He's a blues guitarist from the Mississippi Delta. A town called Asbestos, Mississippi."

"Oh yeah?" asked Maunsel. "A real Delta blues man?"

"Yeah. He's 80 years old but nobody really knows for sure. He only has two fingers. He's a genius," she added.

"Two fingers total or two fingers on one hand?" asked Maunsel, being tiresomely specific.

"They didn't say. I guess it's just two fingers on one hand."

"Would that be two fingers on his picking hand or two fingers on his fret board hand?" Maunsel was creeping dangerously into an attitude of satirical cruelty.

"What?" She was getting defensive. *Time to bail and try an easier question.*

"Where did he get the name 'Train Smoke'

Henry Hitchcock?"

"He is supposed to have a big penis. Supposably, it's longer than 'train smoke,' as they say in the Delta." *She said "supposably." Jesus.*

"Hmmm. Very interesting. I'll see to the tickets. No problem whatsoever," said Maunsel, reassuringly. At this stage it was important to make Haydeé think he had every intention of attending the New Orleans Jazz and Heritage Festival with her and her friends to see the Delta Blues Genius. But there was a 0% chance he would subject himself to such a spectacle: an authentic, common-man performance of indigenous American musical expression before an audience of grungy, white fellow travelers demonstrating their wistful appreciation for the quiet heroics of subsistence laborers playing open-tuned guitars and neck-mounted harmonicas. No thanks. It would hardly interest her to know, Maunsel mused, that the last two songs he downloaded onto his smartphone were Bert Kaempfert's instrumental version of "Canadian Sunset" and "The Theme from Barbarella" by The Glitterhouse. For the moment, the only thing that interested *him* was Kirsten Duplechain's perfect, water balloon tits and their upcoming, afternoon rendezvous at The Watercress. It was time to head downtown.

As he pulled out of the driveway, he convinced himself that he had just enough time to stop on the way to work to buy a lottery ticket. He pulled in to the local Palestinian-run Qwik Stop Mini Mart and took his place in line behind the usual fortune seekers: the poorest black inhabitants of New Orleans waiting like spent electrical vacuum tubes to buy quick-play scratch-off lottery tickets with clever Louisiana-themed names crafted to titillate the lowest possible consumer profile; titles like "Mayhaw Mayhem," "Riverboat Rambler," "Honey Island Hootenanny," "Streetcar Named Retire," "Cochon de Play" and "Wild Pelican" that the clerks would tear from perforated rolls of metallicized cardboard upon request. It was beyond embarrassing to queue up in these bodegas, surrounded by sale racks of white T-shirts and impulse-buy display cases stocked with Phillies strawberry blunts, Al Capone sweet cigars, incense, car deodorizers (cookie-cut from light-gauge cardboard in the shape of cartoon Christmas trees), fragrance oils, air fresheners, glass smoking pipes, black nylon skull covers, lighters, energy drinks, pepper spray, pre-paid cell phones, pre-paid credit cards, fake flowers in slender glass test tubes, playing cards, stash trays, smoker cozies, brass pipe screens, black automotive hose repair tape, dried meat snacks, WIC, EBT and SNAP signs, fake Fraternal Order of Police stick-ons, static cling window lettering kits — all the accoutrements and regalia of urban mischief. In front of him stood a black woman with chemically straightened hair wearing a skin-tight, bulging, pink T-shirt airbrushed with a memorial for a young girl killed by a stray bullet on the front porch of her grandmother's Central City cottage during a drug-related drive-by. It read: "R.I.P. Inesa Fulgence" in light blue lettering beneath an iron-on photograph of a black toddler suspended in gray clouds and surrounded by purple unicorns. The woman was speaking unintelligibly on her smartphone in apparent violation of the hand-written sign posted on the customer side of the cash register that read: "NO TALKING ON CELL

PHONES WHILE BEING SERVED." She terminated her call just in time to avoid reprimand and presented two dollar bills to the brown-skinned, mustachioed cashier who tore off two scratch-off lottery tickets and sent the woman on her way. Maunsel paid ten dollars for five quick-pick Power Ball lottery number combinations and followed her out of the store. The ride to work would only take 15 minutes.

Chapter 4
Irish Channel

FARTHER DOWNTOWN THAT morning, Gretchen Sobieski awoke to the sounds of a garbage truck activating its hydraulic trash compaction press and the whistles of garbage men signaling that it was clear for the driver to proceed on the morning route. Gretchen lived in a 1900s weather board maisonette that was a single-family dwelling when first constructed, but was now divided in half into two up-and-down rental apartments. The dwelling was directly across the street from the neighborhood bar, one of dozens that operated in the section of New Orleans known as the Irish Channel. When Gretchen moved to New Orleans after Hurricane Katrina from Buckthorn

Township Pennsylvania, one of Pittsburgh's quasi-suburbs, she chose to live in the Irish Channel for its bohemian character — a character that expressed itself in the numerous taverns that were scattered throughout the district. The neighborhood tavern once served as an important social fulcrum when the Irish Channel emerged as a bedroom community for the nearby Mississippi River wharves in the late 1800s and early 1900s. Though they had long since ceased operations, mortuary buildings seemed almost as numerous as the bars themselves. There seem to be something very immigrant Irish about the neighborhood, which now had the shabby Gothic character Gretchen came to New Orleans to experience. She savored living on the frontier, so to speak, where lower-middle class residences abutted public housing projects and Section 8 badlands: an invigorating atmosphere to live a life from which she had been sheltered in a Pittsburgh suburb by her bourgeois parents. Gretchen had selected the Irish Channel as the launching point of her new, young-adult life that would include a smattering of gutter culture, a little race-mixing, some gentle iconoclasm, de-caffeinated anarchism, free-form poetry, acoustic roots music, climate consciousness, psychotropic mushrooms, a touch of Eastern mysticism, ethnic food and a floating, pantheistic love of nature; in short a veritable harmonic convergence of everything unconventional and irreverent, all played in a minor key. The Irish Channel had it all, and Gretchen was going to be a bona fide Big Easy Bolshevik.

At age 26, Gretchen very seldom took time to reflect on her own childhood spent in the steel industry environs of eastern Pennsylvania. Though her father was Catholic, her mother was some kind of Eastern or Russian Orthodox. Gretchen attended public schools, but her mother enrolled her in Orthodox Carpatho-catechism classes and shepherded her and her brothers and sisters to mass every Sunday. These forced marches made her resent her mother, her mother's family and organized religion in general. Gretchen was aware that the beauty of the Russian Orthodox service at St. Cyril's church in Buckthorn Township could be a source of satisfying and even aesthetic reflection, but she had deliberately abandoned all that for the laissez-faire lifestyle and *Wandervogelmystik* of New Orleans. Her father would often say that religion was for women and children.

Gretchen and a classmate from the Beersheba Community College of Uniontown, Pennsylvania, decided to move to New Orleans together and were immediately drawn to the Irish Channel neighborhood. Every aspect of city living was accessible to them on foot or on bicycles, and the apartment they rented on Philip Street proved to be a perfect headquarters for the way they wanted to live. Soon enough, they were spending as much time at their neighborhood saloon, Victor's, as they were in their own apartment. Victor's was everything they imagined a neighborhood bar should be: dark, smoky, smelly, with almost no rules, dog friendly, and served by a jukebox that played all kinds of obscure rock and rhythm and blues music from P. J. Proby to the Haystack Hi-Tones. The bartenders were themselves transplants from other parts of the country searching for the same sort of life Gretchen dreamt about. The bond between Gretchen and Victor's staff was established very quickly.

The clientele was as motley as the jukebox selection: aging hippies, un-papered Hispanic construction workers, small-time drug dealers, tattoo artists, service industry nighthawks, black hustlers, biker chicks, crunchy/earthy nature girls, ex-college football players, business casual professionals, federal administrative workers, homosexuals, video poker addicts, menthol cigarette addicts, macramé craftsmen, graffiti artists, automobile mechanics, part-time prostitutes, an old Negro mesmerist who claimed he could hypnotize hens into laying double-yolked eggs and every manner of street corner philosopher imaginable. Gretchen often reflected with great satisfaction that she was an embedded component of this glorious menagerie. When money was low, she could run a tab with any of Victor's bartenders. They would also receive packages when she could not be home to accept them. It was a kind of romanticized hardscrabble utopia.

Better still was the fact that it came with an exhilarating tincture of risk as there was a housing project approximately eight blocks away. Black boys who lived there, or perhaps were temporarily based there, would, from time to time, pillage the nearby Irish Channel neighborhood on nighttime raids when places like Victor's presented attractive opportunities. To Gretchen's way of thinking, these were tolerable nuisances that made living the lifestyle even more authentic. Besides, the poor black children were almost *entitled* to harvest a few smartphones on occasion given the hopelessness of their destitution and the insurmountable impediment of the racist oppression to which they were subject. As long as nobody got hurt, Gretchen could accommodate the inconvenience of petty crimes in her broadening, progressive world view. Besides, providing assistance to the disenfranchised poor was part of her job.

Gretchen was employed by a nonprofit outreach organization known as Empower the Planet, an experimental division of an international recycling interest that targeted blighted urban areas for education in the use of sustainable materials in the construction and repair of low-cost housing; specifically, eco-friendly sheetrock or drywall. Her office was on

Magazine Street, also in the Irish channel, but closer to the much rougher residential areas served predominantly by federal Section 8 housing vouchers. The apartments and other dwellings she called upon were all owned by negligent absentee landlords with whom she never had any contact. As a result, Gretchen dealt directly with the actual residents of these households and could boast that she was delivering valuable services to the real nitty-gritty denizens of the slums. She had come to know many of these families personally, all black and all single-mother households. She could never be sure that the underlying message of ecological responsibility she tried to convey was completely understood by her clientele, but they certainly seemed willing enough to accept any measure of home improvement offered to them.

On this particular morning, Gretchen was assigned to pay an outreach call on a Chippewa Street family that her supervisor discovered had sustained severe drywall damage from a malfunctioning hot water heater. Ms. Wanda Videau and her children lived there in a three bedroom, two bath apartment.

According to the Staff Report Crisis Sheet, a large section of the kitchen wall had become waterlogged and had peeled inward completely off the wooden studs. The insulation blankets were also soaked with water and had descended to floor level. This meant extensive rat and roach infestation and an inability to keep the apartment cool. Gretchen's mission would be to survey the damage, take measurements for replacement materials and provide reassurance to the Videau family that installation of a new wall was on the way. In accordance with her institution's mission, she would also take the opportunity to instruct or advise the family on the benefits of recycling and the value of environmentally responsible energy efficiency. This is exactly what she had come to New Orleans to do.

Before departing for her field work, Gretchen decided to call her new love interest, Jupiter Mingo. She had been on two dates with him by then, and they had made love on the second. Nevertheless, she felt that the relationship was at the stage where the boy should be calling the girl and not the other way around. She acknowledged to herself that such a rule of thumb was old-fashioned, but it just seemed natural that Jupiter should pursue and she withdraw, if only in a perfunctory way. She gave herself a light reprimand for considering the fact that Jupiter was black in formulating her plan for this burgeoning courtship. But there was no way around it – Jupiter was black.

The fact that Jupiter was black was actually a source of titillation. It fit perfectly inside her idea of diversely textured bohemian adventure, and she loved the way people looked at them when they were together. On the other hand, Gretchen was concerned that her attraction to Jupiter was misplaced, that her feelings of affection towards him were based on superficial novelty. She also wondered whether Jupiter's feelings for her were similarly artificial, whether he liked her because he wanted to be seen with her as an act of defiance. *Was Jupiter searching for some kind of external validation (or even condemnation) from the outside world by challenging convention with a mixed-race couple? Was Jupiter energized by society's reaction, good or bad, to a flagrant display of race mixing?* She tried to suppress these feelings. She hated that they bubbled up inside her. At the same time, she was proud that she could overcome them and give herself over to a man, whatever his race may be, for whom she had genuinely romantic feelings.

For God's sake, this is the most tender, intelligent, educated, thoughtful and polite boyfriend I have ever had! He is unlike any black man, dammit, any man I have ever dated! We like the same food, the same music, the same political and cultural heroes and he is absolutely, physically gorgeous. Fuck it if he's black. I'm going to make a full-fledged run at this. She envisioned him in the twilight with his greyhounds.

Gretchen was not going to lose heart as this stage of the relationship, like she had so many times before when unnerved at the thought of commitment. Everything was falling into place for her in this New Orleans experiment. She wasn't going to jeopardize it by being hesitant with Jupiter. When she reflected on their night of lovemaking, there was no sense of creeping regret or embarrassment that she often experienced after meaningless sex. She considered that a favorable sign and gave herself the go-ahead to carry on. She actually felt safe in bed with Jupiter. So safe, in fact that she even engaged in pornographic fantasy when she and Jupiter were apart. Suddenly, she had an irresistible desire to hear Jupiter's voice. But there was work to be done.

Just outside the Empower the Planet facility on Magazine St., Gretchen folded up her Staff Report Crisis Sheet, inserted it into one of the slim compartments in her purse and removed her smartphone. She searched for Jupiter's name in the device's "Contacts" directory and called him via speed dial. Jupiter answered after one ring tone.

"Hi, baby," said Jupiter. Then she heard some garbled words caused by a bad connection.

"Jupiter? Can you hear me?" More garbled words as she began to pace around with a bent head trying to improve the reception.

"Why don't we meet at Victor's for happy hour? Can you hear me? We have a bad connection."

"That'll be fine." She heard his response but then the phone went dead. She was not sure that the aborted conversation matched the lovesick poutiness she was feeling. But Gretchen kept faith and turned her attention to her field call and the pleasures she took in her new bike. It was a one-speed Huffy Cranbrook Dreamcycle with 26" wheels with whitewall tires and a handlebar mounted basket. She kept the heavily padded leather seat extra low so her feet could reach the ground easily at stops even though a low-slung seat meant sacrificing maximum power when underway.

Brimming with expectation, Gretchen straddled her bicycle in a standing position and prepared to set off for her field call on the Videau family. As she placed the ball of her left foot on the rubber pedal to begin her short sortie, she heard the voice of a young man as he emerged from the offices of Empower the Planet. It was Dennis McKinley, her supervisor, a 35-year-old missionary from Emporia, Kansas, who had been assigned to the New Orleans branch after Hurricane Katrina and who had interviewed Gretchen only months earlier for her associate position. He was almost breathless:

"Gretchen! I didn't hear you leave! So, you're

headed for your first CSO?"

"Yup." Gretchen knew CSO stood for "Client Service Outreach," one of the dozen or so abbreviations and acronyms the organization used in the handbooks and flyers and service forms and other printed materials that were available in piles all over the office and even in her apartment. "Going to check on Wanda Videau and family. I'm a little behind schedule. Is there something you need or need to tell me?"

"No, no, not at all! Just wanted to wish you luck and see if you need anything from me, you know, so you're all set?"

"Yup. I'm all set. Shouldn't be gone longer than an hour."

"Excellent, excellent. Listen, Gretchen, I was wondering, if you didn't have anything going on later, if you were busy, whether we could meet somewhere after work, for coffee, or something, and talk about next week's agenda and stuff, you know, I mean, so we can be ready for next week's slate of CSO's."

Gretchen's brain switched from Community Activist mode to Female Target mode in an instant.

This guy was hitting on her. Dennis was looking to spend some after-hours social time. She knew she had to stifle this guy's enthusiasm before he got any ideas. "Oh, damn, Dennis. I've already made plans. I'm available first thing tomorrow morning. We could meet in the conference room first thing. I wish you would've told me earlier." Gretchen chose these words very carefully in order to deliver the unmistakable signal that she didn't want to spend any personal time with Dennis, that she considered any discussion of client services a work-related matter to be handled strictly on office premises.

"Oh, sure, I just thought, I mean, we could get a head start somewhere, you know, away from the phones and all the office chaos."

"I could get here extra early before things get too hectic if you want." Gretchen was certain that her message was being delivered with complete perspicuity. She wanted to tell him that she had a boyfriend and that his name was Jupiter and that he was black and that he was fifty times cooler than Dennis could ever hope to be. But blurting all that out would be too personal. Besides, it was tactically unnecessary. That much he understood.

"Oh, sure, we could do that. Oh, wait. I've got a conference call with the corporate people. I tell you what, I'll come see you after that and see how your schedule looks for the rest of the day."

Gretchen had achieved total shutdown with a flick of her wrist. Having a Jupiter boyfriend sure did come in handy. Not only was it fun to think about as a romance, but it had all kinds of useful applications.

"Sounds good," she said, very professionally. "We'll talk then." With that, Gretchen sprung to the balls of her feet on the rubber pedals of her Dreamcycle and rolled off to fulfill her destiny with the coin of Jupiter Mingo slipped into her heart's treasury. She wondered why the sun was not shining more brightly.

Chapter 5
New Student Orientation

WITH   MISSION   MERCEDES accomplished and Demon Embarrassment in check for the moment, Shale Gimmel guided his silver Cadillac XTS with the black leather interior out of the Monaco Motor Cars parking lot and turned his attention to the emergency Board of Governors meeting called by the president of Tulane, David Kaminsky. The Asian American Students' Union was making noises about the term "orientation" and its connotations of "strangeness" and "maladjustment." It all seemed a bit silly to Shale, not unlike the time a group of African-

American students complained about Gibson Hall and its eponymous honoree, a distinguished General in the Army of the Confederacy. That group had also threatened to boycott classes and occupy administration offices. The university brass offered to build out an (effectively separatist) African-American recreation room next to the cafeteria, so the controversy died down quietly. But the Asian students figured to be a bit more hidebound in their protest. A Board of Governors meeting would have to be convened.

Because Shale was one of the few local New Orleanians who sat on Tulane's Board, Kaminsky begged him to attend this particular meeting. Shale knew that most of the other board members, who lived outside of the New Orleans area in cities from coast to coast including New York, Miami, Los Angeles, Chicago and Dallas, would be attending by means of teleconference. The only local members who were sure to attend were Pokey Melville (short for "Pocahontas"), the local director of the American Civil Liberties Union, and Bartholomew Dolliole, a Creole of color whom Shale knew to be the token black on the Board, though his broad, flat face and silky, curly black hair made him look, it seemed to Shale, more like an Aleutian Indian or some kind of steppe Mongolian. Pokey Melville showed up at every board meeting involving anything even remotely political in nature. Bartholomew Dolliole showed up at absolutely every single meeting to collect the $1500 honorarium payable only upon personal attendance. As Kaminsky explained it to Shale, it wouldn't look good to the rest of the Board if only those members appointed for image purposes, not because they were fund-raising rainmakers, actually attended in person. Kaminsky implored Shale to attend to avoid this embarrassment. Shale's presence would somehow legitimize the muster. After all, Shale gave as much money or more to the University as had any of the national board members even though they were captains of industry in cities with real American economies.

As Shale turned on to McAlister Drive, the main artery of Tulane's campus, he knew there would be parking problems. On regularly scheduled board meetings, the administration would have had time to place traffic cones in front of the prime parking spots to allow board members easy access to the Lavin-Bernick Center where the Stibbs Conference Room was located. At that hour, it was about 1:30 PM, campus was packed with cars and Shale had to find a spot on the other side of Willow Street in the five-story parking garage that served the Wilson Athletic Center. It would be quite a walk back to the Lavin-Bernick Center, which overlooked the main quadrangle at the center of campus. Heavy sweating was sure to be involved, so Shale felt it advisable to wipe off any remaining base makeup he had applied earlier. He parked his car on Level 3 and took the elevator down to the ground floor to begin his slog to the center of campus.

In spite of the heat, Shale made it quickly enough to the entrance of the student center, took the elevator to the second floor and walked to the door of the Stibbs Conference Room. David Kaminsky greeted him immediately with an expression of relief and a slightly frantic handshake. The conference room was enormous. The conference table was enormous. It was the size and shape of the Kansas City Chiefs scoreboard at Arrowhead Stadium. At one end of the table sat Bartholomew Dolliole, the Creole of color who was $1500 richer, and at the other sat Pokey Melville in a brownish pant suit texting on her smart phone. Shale thought she looked slightly more attractive than she did at the last Board meeting. She had let her crew cut grow out and made a modest attempt to darken her now shoulder length gray hair. Instead of the pin prick earrings Shale remembered, she was wearing slightly more feminine gold dew drop earrings and had abandoned the boxy sports jacket, cargo pants and barge boots with gum lug soles. Though she was seated, Shale imagined that she might even have on heels, however low they might be. To Shale's way of thinking, Pokey seem to have abandoned the rugged, lumberjack get-up she had thrown together ever so casually in the past.

A fantasy took hold and began to expand. Each glance at Pokey seemed to last longer and longer. *Perhaps I could walk her to her car after the meeting ended. Perhaps I could ask her to have coffee, or even a drink. Maybe she would like to take a tour of my new hotel. No, scratch that. I need a more socially conscious pretext for a spontaneous pairing. How about abstract expressionist art? I can't take her to a museum, dickhead! I've got to feed her my liberal credentials somehow! Where can I take her and accidentally run into some of my black friends? Oh shit! My pancake makeup! I've wiped it all off! Wait a minute. It is better this way. Pokey would consider makeup vain and shallow. She doesn't even wear makeup. Better, for now, to get back to business and wait for a more propitious opening.*

Shale nodded in a businesslike way to his fellow board members in attendance and they all turned to Kaminsky for some sign that the meeting would commence.

Kaminsky spoke: "Thank you all for showing up on such short notice. The rest of the Board, or at least a respectable number of them, will be participating *via* teleconference. We should hear from them on the speakerphone shortly."

Shale looked to the center of the giant oval

table. Propped up on four padded feet was a circular electronic device with telephone cables draining from various of its portals. It was a space-age piece of equipment made of black and silver plastic with red, green and white blinking lights. It looked like a scale model of one of Blofeld's submersible ocean outposts in a 1980's James Bond movie or even the Bulgarian Communist Headquarters on Mount Buzludzha. Before long, the extraordinary machine began beeping as each of the conference callers joined.

Once the beeping subsided, Kaminsky spoke again: "Thanks everyone for joining us on such short notice. I don't expect this meeting will take too long but the Board needed to be kept apprised of some recent developments that could put a wrinkle in the start of classes for the school year." Shale turned his gaze from the speakerphone to Bartholomew Dolliole who smiled politely. Shale then quickly glanced at Pokey Melville who did not smile. "Uh-oh," thought Shale. "Pokey's got serious business on her mind."

Kaminsky, as President, took over: "Before we get started, why don't we take a quick roll call so everyone knows who is participating." Kaminsky proceeded to recite the list of names from a sheet of paper he held nervously in his hands.

Shale knew most of these men, and two women, one way or another, from business dealings or social occasions or professional basketball-related activities. The sounds of their names brought him back to his childhood days on Dryades Street before his family and other merchant families got rich enough to make the *hegira* out of the Dryades Street area to the suburbs of Lakewood South and Lakewood North, subdivisions developed on the property once occupied by New Orleans' primarily Jewish country club.

Kaminsky got down to business: "The reason I called this emergency meeting is to brief the Board on an ongoing protest by some of our students concerning our freshmen, excuse me, new student orientation program. I might say our 'new student acclimatization' program since it is the word 'orientation' that is causing the problem."

Someone said, "What the hell?" through the speakerphone.

"Nevertheless, the Asian-American students Union has a problem with our use of the word because, according to them, it presupposes that freshmen, pardon me, new students who are confused or overwhelmed by or otherwise unfamiliar with college life associate those feelings with being in the 'Orient' or Asia. The AASU finds it offensive that any foreign land, in other words, any land that is not the United States of America, is considered just that, 'foreign,' or perhaps sub-standard in a way that requires some sort of rehabilitation upon arrival here at Tulane." Someone said, "Jesus H. Christ" over the speakerphone. Bartholomew Dolliole fought back a smile. Pokey Melville uncrossed her legs, shifted in her chair and scowled.

Kaminsky soldiered on: "Now, I know I've sent everyone *via* email a copy of this, but I'd like to read the document out loud for the record, even though we're not on the record, for everyone's consideration and to make sure that we're all on the same page, so to speak. It's a letter or memorandum addressed to me, David Kaminsky, as president of Tulane and to the

Board of Governors. It is from Kahlil Mifsud and Satyavrat Gupta on behalf of the Asian-American Students Union of Tulane University."

"Holy shit," thought Shale, "he's going to read the entire manifesto."

Kaminsky continued: "It reads as follows: 'We, the members of the Asian-American Students Union, hereby lodge a formal objection to that portion of the fall semester initiation activities program entitled "Tulane New Student Orientation." The term "orientation" is offensive to those of us of Asian-American ancestry insofar as it presumes that newcomers to the University are uncomfortable, befuddled or lack the necessary skill set to cope with the university experience and that such difficulties are associated with the 'Orient,' as the Asian area of the world is known by racist, sexist, chauvinist and xenophobic westerners. The shameful practice of white, western discrimination, exploitation, marginalization and condescension visited upon people of Asian descent should not be endorsed by your administration. We call upon you and all others in positions of putative power to cease and desist these perfidies and demand that the "Tulane New Student Orientation" program be re-titled immediately. Should the administration fail to take these corrective measures, the AASU, and all other student organizations traditionally victimized by such officially sanctioned oppression, including the African American Students Union, the Black Student Alliance, the Hebrew Students Union, and the LGBTQ Student Union, all of whom hereby adopt this expression of dissatisfaction, will be forced to undertake a formal protest and physically occupy your offices until our demands are met. Please submit your written response to the above-referenced address within 48 hours of receipt of this correspondence. Respectfully submitted,' *et cetera* and so forth."

The speakerphone crackled with unintelligible turbulence. Kaminsky looked at Shale with a wrinkled nose. Shale puffed up his cheeks and exasparated. Eventually, one of the conference callers was able to break through: "What the hell is LGTQB or whatever the hell you just said?"

Pokey Melville was at the ready: "That's LGBTQ and it stands for lesbian, gay, bisexual, transgendered and queer."

The speakerphone crackled again: "Doesn't 'gay' cover all of that? And what about 'queer?' What the hell is that?"

Pokey Melville started to launch into an explanation, Shale presumed, of the nuanced differences among all of those classifications. He also wondered why "queer" rated a separate listing. It occurred to Shale that the gay community was expressing a certain kind of confidence by expropriating a term used with opprobrium and trumpeting it unabashedly, as in "We're queer, we're here, get over it." The term "queer," he supposed, was an adaptable enough epithet not quite as difficult for the homosexual community to embrace as "fairy" or "dyke."

But Kaminsky, who seemed to sense that the discussion was veering off course into an area even more fraught with stickiness than the "orientation" question, interrupted Pokey and tried to gather the meeting together. He raised his voice slightly: "Let's try and concentrate on the business at hand. Do we want to respond and if so how? You will all be interested to know that every major university in America, and even most smaller colleges, implement programs known as 'New Student Orientation.' The title of the program was not intended to offend anyone. Much of the program is already underway for this semester. Brochures, signs and T-shirts are already being displayed all over campus. I'm not sure we could put the toothpaste back in the tube even if we wanted to. I am sensitive to their feelings but I'm not sure that by changing the title we would be able to deliver to them any satisfaction."

Shale was beginning to see the humor in this awkward meeting and hoped that he would find Bartholomew Dolliole suppressing another conspiratorial smile. But Bartholomew slouched so far down in his chair that he was almost under the gigantic conference room table. Pokey Melville actually took a seat in a different chair to be closer to the speakerphone. President Kaminsky, who was already standing, dropped his head and braced himself with outstretched hands and locked elbows on the back of a nearby chair.

The speakerphone crackled once more: "This is ridiculous. We spent over three quarters of a million dollars last year funding these organizations, and for what? So they can beat us over the head with their screwball demands? We already changed it from 'Freshmen' to 'New Students.' What happens when the news media get hold of this? We're going to have a serious public relations problem on our hands without having done anything wrong!"

"For the Board's information," said President Kaminsky solemnly, "the memorandum was carbon copied to the local newspaper and all four television stations, plus the mayor's office."

"Oh, that's just great," said an unidentified voice from the speakerphone. "I'm trying to run business here in New York and I've got to deal with this foolishness?"

Still another voice from the speakerphone: "Why can't we just tell them what they want to hear, that we'll change the name of the program, that it will take some time to reissue all the literature and such where the name appears and hope the whole thing will blow over."

A more measured voice came through the speakerphone: "Why not look at this as an opportunity? We can be the first institution in the United States to demonstrate their progressive attitudes towards these things and get a little credit for once. Reissuing the literature is a fairly simple matter and, in the grand scheme of things, amounts to only a *de minimus* cost. We can respond in writing within 24 hours, or 48 hours whatever it is, give our assurance that corrective measures will be taken and move on to the next crisis."

Pokey Melville was not going to let this opportunity slip away: "I think it's important that we take an official position in sympathy with the AASU and set out in writing that we have taken an inventory of our transgressions for the purpose of moving the University in a more sensitive direction. For example . . ."

Before Pokey could begin her itemization of

those transgressions, the speakerphone positively erupted: "There is no way in hell I'm going to sit on this Board and authorize an admission of guilt to a stitched-up, trumped-up charge of racial discrimination. If we're going to change the name of the program, fine. If we wanna issue a written statement within 48 hours indicating our intention to do so, fine. But an admission of guilt is out of the question."

As the conference room buzzed with the harumphing and bickering of the Board, Shale felt a blanket of comfort and contentment descend over him as if he were watching a horror movie from the safety of a plush velvet theater seat. He almost smiled. At long last, somebody other than him was facing a troublesome set of circumstances. There is a sense of comfort, Shale reflected, that comes with the news that others are suffering heartburn.

"Listen, Fellas." A new voice from the speakerphone was breaking in. "Does anyone know anything about these two, uh, Asian students? They don't sound Asian to me. I mean, has anyone bothered to check them out? Their names don't sound like they are Chinese or Japanese or whatever. Are they legitimate? Are they instigators from the fringe? You know, who are they?" Shale very well knew that the protesters could not be Vietnamese or Japanese or Korean: Those students were more concerned with making their grades and securing their futures; after all, resolute ambition is never distracted by anserine petulance or sophomoric righteousness on its way to personal achievement. The Gimmelfarb escutcheon, if there was one, would surely bear the same motto.

Pocahontas Melville was about to jump through the speakerphone. But Kaminsky pre-empted: "No, no, no, no they are exemplary individuals, fine students. Let's not stick our hands in that tar . . . Let's not go off the reservation, here. This is a serious complaint requiring a serious response." *Holy fuck, he almost said "tar baby." And replaced it with a slur against Native Americans! There's a woman named Pocahontas Melville sitting in this very meeting! Why not throw in "African American Engineering" and "Chinaman's Chance" while you're at it!* Pokey found an opening: "These students deserve our utmost respect! They've shown great courage in bringing this travesty to our attention. And this isn't the only injustice perpetuated by Tulane, as such."

The speakerphone erupted again. Shale was beginning to enjoy himself. It was like watching a fistfight break out at a South Korean National Assembly meeting, a real slapstick *mêlée*. Kaminsky massaged his temples. Pokey folded her arms and paced. Bartholomew Dolliole peered at the inside of his empty coffee cup. Shale tried to think of something to say. This was the perfect time to come to Pokey's aid, to support her position, to validate her concerns, to flirt.

"It seems to me that Miz (*careful*) Melville has a point. We don't want to whitewash these people (*oops*). We've got to acknowledge, at least on some level, that the title was, at the very least, insensitive. I think her concerns are worth considering, in fact, should actually *be* considered in formulating our response."

As Shale expected, the speakerphone buzzed and rattled with indignant concerns voiced by various

Board members, but he didn't pay attention. He looked over at Pokey and hoped for a thankful reaction, an acknowledgment that they were *simpatico*. Perhaps even a smile. But there was nothing. Pokey never took her eyes off the speakerphone. *Great. I've compromised my solidarity with the important members of the Board with a clumsy overture to an oblivious prospect.* Demon Embarrassment took a seat on his left shoulder and reminded him that he was exposed with no makeup.

Shale placed the palm of his right hand over his closed mouth and dug his thumb into the joint of his mandible. As he glanced towards the center of the conference room table, he could see that Pocahontas Melville had spun away from the speakerphone and was walking towards him. He tried not to look at her as she approached, but he could not ignore it when she stopped immediately beside his chair and bent down as if to whisper in his ear. He removed his hand from his face and leaned forward with his forearms on the conference room table in an attitude of accommodation so as to signal to her with his body language that he was ready to listen attentively. He tried not to swallow as her hair brushed against his cheek and her breath made the hair in his ears rustle. She spoke *sotto voce*:

"Why don't we make a motion to reconvene this meeting until we can gather more facts? These guys are obviously not inclined to deal with this problem seriously right now. If we had more time, maybe they would cool off and be more willing, later on, to go along with a more sensitive response plan. Don't you agree?"

As Pokey backed away from the side of his head to see his response, Shale felt a flash of excitement come over his face. *The overture worked! We are going to be conspirators! We are going to be confederates in a tactical caper!* Fearing it was best not to speak lest his voice crack, Shale looked up at Pokey's spectacular face and nodded.

She smiled, and began to whisper in his ear once again: "Why don't you and I go down to the cafeteria so we can speak alone. You and I can craft a responsible course of action and present it to the Board later. By that time, who knows, the students may have begun their protest. The board will not be able to withstand that kind of pressure."

Shale's heart almost burst through his chest. The prospect of a private consultation with Pokey at a corner table in the Tulane cafeteria was just too fantastic. His mind raced. He had to figure out a way to get out of this meeting cleanly without embarrassing President Kaminsky in front of the rest of the Board. This getaway was going to require a certain amount of finesse.

At that very moment, his smart phone buzzed in his pants pocket alerting him to an incoming text message from his garage manager at The Watercress. He removed his phone discreetly and held it under the table so that no one, especially Pokey, who was hovering feverishly over him, could see his preoccupation. The preliminary text message indicator flashed a red triangle with a yellow exclamation point inside it informing him that there was an emergency. The text message read as follows: "Your girlfriend just arrived. Parked white Mercedes in reserve spot. Was with young man. May wanna get down here."

Shale felt his face burning. His field of vision went white. Thoughts of the Pocahontas Conspiracy vanished. *Der mentsh trakht un Got lakht.*

He stuffed his phone back in his pocket and stood up. "David, I mean, Mr. President, I have an emergency. You'll have to excuse me." As he hustled to the door of the conference room, the bickering continued. Pocahontas Melville stood as she watched Shale fly for the door, her mouth open and her eyes blinking. But Shale did not notice.

Chapter 6

Mop Up

BY 9:45 AM, JUPITER MINGO HAD reached his streetcar destination at the corner of St. Charles Avenue and Jackson Avenue. He had one block to walk to reach the intersection of Josephine Street where The Watercress stood. The employee entrance was on the side of the hotel on Josephine. There was a short, enclosed alleyway or tunnel that led to the interior of the building where a shipping and receiving clerk could eyeball visitors, employees and delivery personnel through a wire-reinforced window and buzz them in through the adjacent metal door when appropriate. As Jupiter reached the window at the end of the alley way, he nodded at the clerk who recognized him and a buzzing sound signaled that the door bolt had retracted. He proceeded to the locker room where he stored his backpack, slipped on his black and white checked gingham kitchen pants and a white T-shirt. He fondled his smartphone and considered sending a text to Gretchen that might proclaim his feelings for her. *Maybe it's too soon. Oh, fuck it. I'm jumping in. No, wait a minute. At least send something affectionate! Here goes.* He thumbed in a text and pressed "Send." It read: "Can't stop thinking boutcha!" *That overture should send the right signal. Waiting for her answer is going to be maddening!* There was no immediate response. He tried not to panic. *Was she giving him some kind of signal?* He had to finish dressing. The last piece of his uniform was a pressed, but not starched, apron kept in a storeroom with similarly laundered tablecloths and napkins, all sorted in neat stacks on metal shelves.

He entered the kitchen through a door adjacent to the storeroom and stood before a piece of equipment that he would be operating for the next seven hours: a stainless steel, all-in-one commercial dishwashing station. It was a one-man assembly-line system that worked from left to right as you faced it. The whole contraption looked like something Charles Sheeler would paint. The first station, at the far left, was a two-foot square stainless steel counter surface with curved, two-inch edges where cooks assistants would place pots, pans, skillets and a variety of kitchen utensils, all made of aluminum and all encrusted with drying food. The busboys would place dirty plates, glasses and flatware on the same surface after use by diners. The next station, to the immediate right of the steel countertop, was a large, one basin sink over which dangled a rubberized, multi-directional faucet equipped with a hand-activated, spring-loaded spray nozzle. The system was designed so that, at this station, a dishwasher could conduct a preliminary rinsing of the dirty items before placing them on square, rubber-coated, plastic dishwashing racks for processing in the next station — an automatic, self-soaping, jet propulsion dishwasher with internal nozzles that sprayed super-heated water. Both the left and right sides of the stainless steel box enclosing this automatic system would rise and descend, as necessary, when the operator lifted or drew down on the horizontal handles attached to either side. When the washing cycle was complete, Jupiter would slide the plastic racks out from under the metal box and on to another 2-foot square metal countertop where the cleaned items would briefly drip dry and then be wiped for storage and re-use.

On this morning, Jupiter noticed that one of the flanges in the pipeline leading to the dishwasher box was loose and sure to disengage. He had warned his kitchen manager and boss, Brandon Cazenave, about this problem several times, but the engineers were never called and the loosening of the flange only got worse. "That motherfucker Cazenave," Jupiter said to himself, "he's gonna let this thing rattle out until the pipe bursts. I'll get sprayed with scalding water and the whole kitchen will flood." *Will Gretchen respond in kind to my text? Will she have second thoughts about dating a black guy?* He decided to notify Cazenave again.

"Hey, Brandon," said Jupiter as the kitchen prepped for the lunch rush. "If you don't get this pipe fixed, were going to have a disaster on our hands."

"Just wash the fucking dishes and I'll worry about the pipes," replied Brandon, asserting his position as Jupiter's superior. Jupiter shook his head silently and returned to his dishwashing post. But his mind began to race. Brandon Cazenave was a typical, light-skinned, Creole black New Orleanian who looked down on his blackest brothers and resented them for retarding a social progression he might have made without the associated taint of the darker phenotypes. Jupiter was keenly aware that Brandon was one of those French-Catholic, mixed-race scions of that in-between issue of white masters and their slave concubines. They all had impossibly French names like Cazenave, Lapeyrolerie, Reimonenq, Dorefeuille, Guimbilotte and Manumishon (somebody's idea of a joke). Jupiter knew they were the kind of names flagged by the Bureau of Vital Statistics in the 1920s for observation as carriers of possible Negro blood. None of these aboriginally white, French names survived in the contemporary white community of New Orleans because French aristocrats, reduced to genteel poverty by 1900, married off their daughters to wealthy, English-speaking Americans of the Garden District and gradually died off. So here was Brandon Cazenave, the walking/talking enfleshment of cracker *plaçage*, imposing his social superiority on Jupiter Mingo, the pure-blooded descendant of African slaves. *I've got a white girlfriend! How do you like that, motherfucker!?!? Or do I?*

Soon enough, the kitchen was holding forth energetically for the lunch seating at "Moss." The hotel restaurant was *ultra-chic* so the place settings were complicated: chargers, dinner plates, butter plates, demitasse coffee cups, saucers, dessert plates, salad plates, soup bowls, dinner forks, steak knives, salad forks, oyster forks, soup spoons, runcible spoons, fish knives, butter knives, crab crackers, lobster picks, caviar spoons, stilton spoons, marrow scoops, wine glasses, champagne flutes, sugar tongs and so forth, all designed, Jupiter had been told, by the creative team of the New York firm, de Stijl. As fancy as all this was, the menu was deliberately minimalist: Instead of prolix descriptions of complicated entrées, the menu merely listed the dishes by category (mutton, beef, fish, poultry, pork, shellfish) with no details whatsoever about how the food was prepared or garnished or seasoned. Furthermore, the waiters were instructed to demur when asked these specifics, signaling to the diners that the preparation of the day's delectations was to be left exclusively to the discretion of the master chefs. Appetizers, salads and desserts were not listed at all on the menu but were simply brought to the table without ever having been ordered. The whole experience at Moss was positively despotic. But Jupiter didn't give a shit.

This pretentious system was strictly policed by the restaurant's *Maître d'hôtel*, the Mexican *weibling*, Fabrizio Mariposa. Although of slight build and delicate features, he was a spitfire, quick to scold staff subordinates and surprisingly voluble when expressing dissatisfaction. He claimed to be Argentine, but Jupiter knew he was really Mexican. Fabrizio had a face like a silver hatchet. But there was, on occasion, a softer aspect to his mien. One day, before his lunch shift began, Jupiter spotted Fabrizio scooping the pollen from the petals of a bouquet of lilacs with his pinky finger and wiping the purple dust on his eyelids as eye shadow. On other occasions, he would slip cash to the black busboys for reasons Jupiter could only surmise. All the same, Fabrizio Mariposa treated Jupiter with contempt and spoke to him only with derision, if at all. Jupiter hated the little Mexican uraniac.

By 1 PM, conditions in the kitchen were absolutely frantic. Chefs were screaming, waiters were protesting, pots were clanging, plates were crashing, but Jupiter Mingo's dishwashing operation was running smoothly. He was mucking the stalls, as it were, with great efficiency, getting the filthy items cleaned, dried and stored as quickly as they came in. But a feeling of uneasiness was beginning to come over him and his rhythm was under threat. From time to time, he would glance at the rattling flange he had had under observation for some time. By 1:15 PM, the screws in the flange were coming loose and the pipes on either side of it were trembling. And just as he started to curse under his breath at Brandon's neglect, the flange broke apart and the pipes separated. Hot water spewed all over the dishwashing area and flowed under the rubber mats on the cooks' hot line where waiters would stand to collect their orders. Pretty soon, water was flowing out of the kitchen door and into the sunken storeroom one step down from floor level. The slope of the kitchen floor and the recessed level of the storeroom gave direction to the water flow, which meant that the storeroom served as a kind of reservoir for the flood.

Jupiter managed to contain, temporarily, the free flow of water from the busted pipe and, at the same time, fulfill his dishwashing responsibilities until lunch ended at around 2:15 PM. Sure enough, Brandon Cazenave came storming over to Jupiter's dishwashing station and began barking out recovery orders: "First of all, Jupiter, go to the storeroom and get some of those napkins and table cloths and start soaking up this water." Menacing shapes were beginning to form before his very eyes: His dishwashing station appeared as a conglomeration of sharpened stakes, metal throwing stars, scythes, razors, barbed wire, pole axes, table saw blades pitons, picks voulges and halberds.

The sort of miscellaneous, metal cannon fodder Napoleon Bonaparte used against rioting Paris mobs on his rise to power. The neurotransmitters of his dorsal anterior cingulated cortex were misfiring.

Jupiter was incredulous: "You want me to use those freshly pressed linens to mop this shit up? Why don't we get a squeegee and push the water through the employee entrance out to the street?"

"Just soak the shit up like I told you so I can get the engineers in here and seal that pipe up," said Brandon, remorselessly late.

"This is fucked up," muttered Jupiter. But, *befehl ist befehl*, so he grabbed two huge stacks of freshly pressed linens and tossed them on the floor wherever he thought they would do the most good. At that very moment, in walked Fabrizio Mariposa.

"What de fark are joo doin'!?" Fabrizio screamed. "Those are my Frette leenens! Who tole joo to jooze my Frette linens to doo dis?" As he looked up from the floor at Fabrizio, Jupiter saw Brandon Cazenave looming behind them both, waiting to hear whether Jupiter would rat him out for giving the wasteful instruction. Jupiter stayed silent, interested to hear whether Brandon would own up to the misadventure, but Brandon said nothing and stood before the pregnant scene without blinking. Fabrizio appeared to him a cross between the portraits of Ambrose Vollard by Picasso and the one of Pope Innocent X by Velasquez. The hallucination was ferocious: The fearsome visage of a foxfiend garroted by a neckpiece of jagged shards from shattered plate glass.

But Jupiter was no snitch. As enough time passed for him to realize that Brandon was not going to come clean, he started into a meek explanation: "It was an emergency. I just thought that something needed to be done before equipment got ruined or somebody got hurt."

"Yoo stoopid leedle sheet! What are we going to do for dee deennar seating tonight!?!?" shrieked Fabrizio, now at the top of his lungs.

Jupiter felt caught between Caliban and Sporus. He had eaten shit for Brandon and was taking the blame for a reckless frolic that was somebody else's idea. A vengeful fury rushed through Jupiter. Brandon's obvious cowardice combined with his glib condescension called for a strong response and Jupiter wanted to teach him a lesson.

"Did you ever get your driver's license?" It was the voice of the beat cop from earlier that morning. The fat police officer in a light blue shirt with scalloped pockets and a utility belt had observed the dressing down Jupiter had caught from Brandon and Fabrizio. With a sarcastic grin, the cop was dipping shrimp into a cup of cocktail sauce and inserting them into his disgusting mouth with an attitude of privilege. "You know, on the driver's license test, they ask you the best way to mop shit up at the scene of an accident. The answer is: 'Not with fresh linens.' And that's one of the easiest questions on the test!"

Jupiter stifled the urge to stuff the cop's meaty head into the stainless steel dishwasher. Apparently, the cop had been detailed to The Watercress on the very day that Jupiter would receive the most unjustified humiliation of his dishwashing career. On top of that, this beat cop seemed to be following Jupiter around. He felt his heart beating hard and his pulse knocking against his temples. His ears even began to ring a little bit. But Jupiter was powerless and, even though he wanted to lash out, was determined to restrain himself — bereft, as he was, of any immediate options. The beat cop licked his fingers after each insertion of shrimp followed by a smug chuckle. Fabrizio and Brandon joined the amusement as a show of solidarity with the officer of like rank at The Watercress.

Jupiter got to his feet, soaking wet, on the floor of the storeroom determined to stay cool. But his equanimity was interrupted by a newsflash broadcast on the employee television monitor bolted to the outside wall of the shipping/receiving office. A reporter was broadcasting live from the University of New Orleans Lakefront Arena. "Seletha Raspberry is live on the scene," the daytime anchorwoman advised. "What can you tell us, Seletha?"

"Thank you, Jennifer. Near riot conditions broke out at the UNO Lakefront Arena at approximately 1:30 PM today, police officials advise us. Hundreds of people were in line to obtain Section 8 vouchers at the Housing Fair sponsored by HANO, that's the Housing Authority of New Orleans. At approximately 1:30, police tell us, shots were fired, although it is unclear at this time whether police fired into the crowd of those lining up to receive vouchers, or whether the shots came from members of the crowd itself. What we can tell you is that there is mass confusion out here. First responders are on the scene to tend to the injured. The total number of injuries is not known at this time but police have told us there is one confirmed death among the Section 8 applicants. Repeat, one confirmed dead. She is being identified as 74-year-old Josephine Boniface, address unknown. Repeat, one confirmed dead, 74-year-old female Josephine Boniface, at a chaotic Section 8 Housing Fair outside of the UNO Lakefront Arena. I'll be back with more as facts become known to us. Jennifer, back to you."

Jupiter Mingo fell to his weakened knees in six inches of water and prepared to vomit. His brain could not process information and his extremities went numb. He thought he heard Brandon Cazenave say: "All right,

Jupiter, get up off the floor and clean this shit up."
Suddenly, Jupiter felt strong enough to stand up. He no
longer felt rage, only a sense of purpose. He stepped
out of the inundated storeroom and marched towards
his locker, his shoes and socks sloshing with every step.
Once again, he checked his smartphone for a response
from Gretchen. He hoped for the solace any word from
her would bring. He decided to resign himself to the
obvious fact that Gretchen wanted to distance herself
from him. There was now nothing left for Jupiter. He
knew what he must do. His time had come.

Chapter 7

Americana!

MAUNSEL WILLIAMS BLACKSHEAR was still at his ergonomic desk staring at side-by-side-by-side computer screens at 12:30 PM, by which time all of his bullpen associates had long since gone to lunch. In his business, the boys ate lunch at 11 AM. You get hungry early when you arrive at 7 AM to start calling on customers. But Maunsel was not working. He was waiting – waiting on his girlfriend, Kirsten Duplechain, to text him word that the afternoon's tryst was confirmed and that she would come to collect him at his office. At 12:32 PM, his smart phone buzzed on his desk with a text message: "Pick u up front of ur bldg in 10 min." Kirstin had arranged for a room at The

Watercress and wanted to show him her new car (provided courtesy of her sponsor, Shale Gimmel). As distasteful as it was, Kirstin was also the mistress of one of New Orleans' wealthiest men, but Maunsel was in no position to cast a cold eye. Besides, he was curious to see how luxurious the rooms at The Watercress were. He had been to the old Pontchartrain Hotel many times as a child to visit his grandmother. She had taken up residence there with a half a dozen other Episcopalian matriarchs to spend their final days playing bridge and befriending their black servants. He remembered watching the waiters in the Caribbean Room dance with flaming trays of Baked Alaska on Carnival day.

Maunsel took the elevator from his office down to street level and scanned on-coming traffic for any sign of a mistress-mobile slowing on approach in the right-hand lane. Moments later, a white Mercedes-Benz C250 Coupe pulled to the curb. The passenger side window descended and a very feminine voice said: "Hop on in!"

"Good-Ness gracious!" exclaimed Maunsel, as

he lowered himself into the tan leather passenger seat. "You weren't fuckin' around when you picked this one out!"

"No, indeed," said Kirstin. "This baby's got everything. Retracting LED video screen. GPS navigation. MP3 media interface. Satellite radio. Voice-activated Bluetooth communication system. Seat warmers. This bad boy is loaded."

Maunsel leaned over as if to kiss her but said: "Can it take us to The Watercress?"

"Ab-sow-LOOT-lee! But first, we have to make a pit stop in Metairie." These are words Maunsel dreaded — not only because sex would be delayed, but because it meant a detour to the white-flight wastelands of Jefferson Parish, the land of giant, inflatable, spasmodic, stick-figure Sky Dancer dummies that beckoned daiquiri drinkers and chiropractic patients in need of automobile title transfers (with plenty of parking!). The thought of it deflated his buoyant mood, but he had to grit his teeth and get it over with. Kirstin put the car in drive and pressed the accelerator pedal firmly with the toe of her high-heeled shoe. Maunsel was thrown back into his leather seat and off they were to the Interstate, a passage to suburbia.

"Where we headed?" Maunsel inquired, hoping the trip would be a quick one.

"To my new favorite restaurant, Americana, to see Angie and pick up a Jugo de Papaya," she replied, referring to one of her roommates, Angela Waguespack, and to one of her favorite frozen juice drinks. "It's made with four kinds of rum. You're gonna love it."

Kirstin Duplechain was from Destrehan, Louisiana, a semi-rural, suburban ranch home development as were her roommates Angela Waguespack and Trisha Chauvin. She was graduated from the University of New Orleans with a major in "Organizational Leadership," a discipline designed to prepare students to "assume leadership positions in cultural and arts institutions." Her parents were C.J. and Krystal Duplechain who still resided in Destrehan. Her father owned Perrodin's Janitorial Supply Company and her mother worked as a civil minute clerk for the 29th Judicial District Court Judge Emile

"Pinky" Sotile ("Sow-teel"). Growing up in Destrehan with that family meant that Kirsten considered a trip to Metairie a cosmopolitan experience. Even though she spent most of her time within the city limits of New Orleans, Kirstin never lost her appreciation for Metairie as a lodestar of sophisticated city life. Metairie was only halfway to New Orleans from Destrehan and you didn't have to worry about black people. Metairie was also an area where she felt safely away from Shale Gimmel who would never be caught dead there. Maunsel tried not to think about Kirsten and Shale together.

Maunsel had been face-to-face with Shale at least once earlier that year at a debutante party. Not just any debutante party, but a real statement debutante party, an extravagant and sumptuous money burn, the kind that would be measured against others of its ilk: Productions with exotic themes likes "An Evening in Monte Carlo" or "The Feast of Tiberius at the Grotto." These whimsical functions were anything but, costing a minimum of $1 million a piece, typically put on by New Orleans ultra-wealthy. The party where Maunsel first met Shale in person was, he remembered, hosted by the Mendenhalls, the parents of a lovely but somewhat overwhelmed college girl. The Mendenhalls were the marital union of North Louisiana or Oklahoma oil money and Mississippi bourgeois Rastignacs grasping for social prominence with the talons of conspicuous consumption. These were not the old families of New Orleans – certainly not Lancaster Club material, as Maunsel would reflect with some satisfaction. Still, Haydée would insist that she and Maunsel attend this spectacular saturnalia because it was an opportunity to promote her Tikkun Olam fundraiser, and not least because it was imperative that they be seen at an event where the plutocracy of New Orleans would be browsing and sluicing. There was an identifiable synapse somewhere in his wife's cerebrum that, when stimulated by this moment's social occasion of the century, would fire. Haydée would make whatever arrangements were necessary to ensure that Mr. and Mrs. Maunsel Williams Blackshear were breathlessly in attendance.

The Mendenhall party where Maunsel and

Shale stood face-to-face was perhaps the most expensive and most anticipated of any that had ever been held in the city. The invitations came to the Blackshear's in a plain cardboard box, five inches by 3 inches by 2 inches, addressed by hand with black ink fountain pen calligraphy. It was so unusual that Maunsel and Haydée made a ritual of opening it together. Such a delight it was to open the strange package! Maunsel experienced a twinge in his scrotum as he and Haydée snuggled closely for the teamwork it took to carefully manipulate the boxcutter along the flap-seams of the small box that were held together with brown, fiber re-inforced packing tape.

"What in the world kind of invitation is this?" Maunsel had asked, confident that his wife would know all the details that were surely in circulation within her juice-box mommy *milieu*.

"The party is being produced by deStijl, the entertainment division of the New York design firm. The production team has been here for the last month. They're all staying at The Watercress."

"Did you say 'produced'? Like a movie or a

Super Bowl half-time show?"

"All these parties have a producer. They're too much for an amateur to coordinate: Dee-Jays, orchestras, warm-up bands, feature artists, models and actors, props, lighting and sets. And that's before you even get to the catering. And then there's transportation and logistics. Wardrobe and makeup for the deb herself and her mother and grandmother. Wardrobe for the father and his lieutenants. You have to hire a professional firm."

"Wow, I guess the firm had a hand in this invitation design as well."

"Oh, definitely. And this will be the first invite of its kind — completely cyber savvy. We're gonna need your laptop to process the invitation from a thumb drive."

As Maunsel went to retrieve his laptop, he had tried to imagine how he could ever make enough money to afford Baby Mathilde's debutante party when she came of age. He couldn't think about that. Besides, he remembered enjoying himself and, strangely, enjoying partnering with his wife in the ceremony of following the electronic invitation instructions. For a significant portion of the ride out to Jefferson Parish, he had forgotten that he was in the middle of a trysting episode with his mistress Kirsten Duplechain in a car purchased by Shale Gimmel himself.

As the Mercedes cruised silently out to Jefferson Parish, the reverie continued as Maunsel recalled the titillating exercise of discovering the wonders the computerized invitation would reveal when he inserted the two-and-one-half inch external hard drive cartridge into the Universal Serial Bus port of his laptop computer. The title page of the cybervite read as follows:

BERILINERLUFT

DANCE ON THE RIM OF THE VOLCANO

AT AN EVENING IN WEIMAR BERLIN

In honor of AINSLEY MENDENHALL

Beneath that message was a line of sub-topics you could click on to explore the details of the party buried deeper in guts of the thumb drive's electronic *corpus*. They read: "HOME – GIVEN BY– TRANSPORTATION – LOCATION –

ADMITTANCE – PARTY LAYOUT – INTERACTIVE – RSVP." The lettering on this homepage appeared to Maunsel to have been written in a commercial font designed by Joseph Albers or Peter Behrens or some other Bauhaus *Koryphäe* from the 1920's German collaborative. The producers of this party seemed, in the true spirit of the Bauhaus, to have thought of every detail.

Maunsel remembered that he and his wife had ticklishly enjoyed playing around with the computerized invitation, soon learning that the cardboard box also contained two adhesive bandages sealed in crimped, white pouches and two battery-operated, hand-held, diamond-tipped vaporizer smoking wands. They had learned by further investigation that the adhesive bandages were embedded with microchips programmed specifically for each of them. The bandages were to be applied to the back of their left hands and then offered on the night of the party for electronic access to the limousine that would transfer guests (six at a time) from the staging area in Audubon Park to the Latter Library on St.

Charles Avenue where the Weimar celebration of Ainsley Mendenhall's *annos nubiles* would be held.

Maunsel remembered beaming at the prospect of socializing at the old Latter Library. He knew that it had been built in the 1900's for a prominent Jewish retailer named Marks Isaacs. It was the only St. Charles Avenue Mansion that still sat on its own undivided city block. Maunsel had guessed that Ainsley Mendenhall's parents must have thrown so much money at the Mayor that he had no choice but to lease out the public library facility to them for the private function. The Mayor would have a political price to pay for allowing white oligarchs to use city property — property that the Black Community considered its exclusive province. As this recollected daydream continued, Maunsel stared out of the passenger side window of the Mercedes sports car as his mistress, Kirsten Duplechain, prattled on her cellular phone with one of her girlfriends about how the Contessa slipped the corset, as it were.

But Maunsel's internal *ruckblick* had more than just nostalgic significance: It was at this Weimarthemed debutante party that he first spoke to Shale Gimmel, his mistress' primary paramour. When he and Haydée exited the limousine at the front gate of the Latter Library on that winter evening only months before, he surveyed the party battlements and marveled at the scaled-down, yet still imposing, fiberglass reproduction of the Brandenburg Gates. Maunsel recognized the handiwork of the Barth Brothers, the Mardi Gras float builders known to all as the most aesthetically accomplished craftsmen in the industry. As they had walked under the ersatz monument, a security guard dressed in a *Sicherheitzpolizei* uniform had passed an electronic wand over their microchip-embedded adhesive bandages and they were waved in. They walked up the driveway painted in large blue letters "RIVER SPREE," and climbed the steps of the main building of the library. Above the exterior of the front door leading to the vestibule, there was a sign in naked white light bulbs that read "RESI." Maunsel had recognized that name from the invitation's flash drive tutorial as the name of the notorious nightclub on Berlin's *Blumenstrasse*. According to the tutorial, The

Resi was a wildly popular cabaret/supper club/dance hall in 1920's Berlin, famous for its lavish décor and libertine clientele. Maunsel remembered pivoting beneath that sign to survey the grounds surrounding the main building. There were at least four tents that had been erected at intervals and connected by canvas sidewalks or pathways. Each tent, big enough to hold fifty or so people, had its own sign announcing the Berlin night club it would represent: the *"Weisse Maus,"* the "Blue Stocking," "El Dorado" and the "Aukula Lounge." Each had its own band and its own specialty motif. Maunsel recalled thinking that he would explore all of these side shows before night's end.

As he and Haydée strolled through the vestibule and into the party, they came upon a 7-foot long glass case where an unshaven, emaciated male actor lay prone. The glass case itself was mounted on a wooden table with hooks hanging down from the soffit of the table ledge. The hooks held a dangling wooden plank with words burned into it that read: "MORPHINE ADDICT STARVING HIMSELF TO DEATH."

Maunsel figured this exhibition was part of an authentic recreation of the depraved entertainment craved by curiosity seekers visiting interbellum Berlin. Maunsel wondered what provisions the actor had made for bladder relief.

As he surveyed the open space of the main building's interior, Maunsel was awestruck. There must have been 350 people sitting at small tables for two or four, dancing on a central hardwood floor, queing up at the cocktail bars staffed by men in white tunics and black bow ties (no women bar tenders, to be historically accurate), loading up China plates monogrammed with Prussian Blue "A.M." at stainless steel buffet trays or standing in little conversation clusters trying to be heard above the raucous din. But louder than all of that was the 24-piece orchestra on a broad mechanically elevated band box holding forth in their full dress (white tie and tails). The elevating machine looked like something that would be used at a Convention center, with two pairs of steel elbows that could be extended to lift the band platform. The band hired for the main building that night was Vince

Giordano and his Nighthawks, complete with a bass saxophone, drum kit with a bass drum frontispiece painted in a Chinese motif, violins, saxophones, cornets, trumpets, trombones and even a vibraphone. The male vocalist stood before one of those chrome-plated, ribbon microphones with wrap-around louvers on a faceguard modeled after the helmet of a Fritz Lang robot. It was the size and weight of a tin of French *mousse truffee*. He seemed to be singing in German but with occasional English words tossed in to convey a sensibility to 20s hepcat slang. The songs had titles like "Kann Denn Libe Sunde Seim" ("Can Love be a Sin?"), "Mir Hab'n Se Hals Geheilt Entlassen" ("I was Released as Cured"), "Erst Trink Mit Mir Ein Bierchen" ("Drink Alcohol With Me") and "Heinrich Wo Grefst Du Denn Hin?" ("Heinrich, Where are You Putting Your Hands?"). The entire room positively throbbed with Jazz Age hedonism. Maunsel remembered that he had felt Haydée's delicate hand slip into his as he escorted her around the Weimar gaiety, and Maunsel was thrilled.

He and Haydée had chatted in desultory fashion

to various Uptown acquaintances as they ordered drinks from one of the bars (scotch-and-soda for him, Pinot Grigio for her). Turning away from the bar into the thick of the revelry, Maunsel saw an older but attractive Jewish lady waving at Haydée from a four-top table where she was seated with an older Jewish gentleman suffering from what seemed like a facial skin condition. The aging *mensch* was peering down at his smartphone, paying no attention to his companion's gesticulations. Maunsel heard the older lady cry: "Haydée! Haydée! Come join us!"

Holy fuckin' shit. It's Shale Gimmel, of all people. She's gonna have me sitting at a table with my girlfriend's Sugar Daddy. Maunsel brought his scotch-and-soda to his face as if to hide behind the glass tumbler. The initial sensations of terror had given him a painful, fuzzy, electrical feeling on his scalp. Haydée pulled at his arm, stopped him in mid-stroll, lifted her face close enough to be private but in a voice loud enough to be heard above the orchestra.

"It's Shale and Millie Gimmel," she said. "He's on the board of the Arts Council and she's on the executive committee of the fundraiser for the Bradford Building. Try not to be sarcastic." The conversation he was to have with the Gimmels at the Ainsley Mendenhall *Berlinerluft* debutante party was one that stuck with him even, as he was then, in Shale Gimmel's Mercedes with Shale Gimmel's mistress traveling to Jefferson Parish on an errand that was to precede an afternoon of sexual congress at Shale Gimmel's hotel. Maunsel remembered that, as the Blackshears sat at the four-top with the Gimmels, Shale would look up from his smartphone at Maunsel and his young wife. Maunsel had wondered if Shale had any reason to recognize him.

"Isn't this fabulous!" said Millie Gimmel, obviously relishing the thought of being at such a blowout and perhaps, thought Maunsel, of being seated with members of a social class that ordinarily did not mix with Jews.

"Did you enjoy playing around with the electronic invitation?" continued Millie. "You see these pneumatic tubes? There's one at every table!" Maunsel examined the swan-necked fixture that curled over the table covered in a white cotton cloth. It seemed to be connected to a system of delivery tubes that shot up overhead and snaked around the interior space of the Latter Library. The contraption made periodic swooshing and sucking noises. The system of tubes was similar to the ones used by banks with drive-thru windows, where business was conducted (check cashing, savings deposits, *etc*.) between tellers behind glass and drivers in their cars taking advantage of the convenience.

Millie continued, with her remarks primarily directed to Haydée: "It's just like the nightclub in Berlin – The Resi! It's short for 'Residenz-Casino' and they've even rigged up the pneumatic tube system."

Haydée took the bait and flattered Millie by asking for further enlightenment: "What are they for?"

"At The Resi in 1920's Berlin, the tube system was offered for patrons to flirt with one another by sending little favours and trinkets directly to their tables. Isn't it fabulous!" Millie practically had to scream to be heard above the music and roar of the celebration, but she was succeeding. Maunsel would occasionally glance at Shale, but he seemed completely uninterested in anything taking place at their awkward little gathering.

"What is it that we're supposed to send to our flirt-mates," asked Haydée in furtherance of her deference to Millie's eagerness to display her appreciation of the obscure party-theme.

"You see the girls with the trays hanging from their necks? The ones that look like cigarette girls? Those trays are stocked with little gifts you can purchase. Little vials of perfume, playing cards, cigar cutters, flavored liquids for your vapor cigarette sticks. They fit inside these little cartridges that you shoot to other tables."

Maunsel chimed in unexpectedly: "You have to *purchase* these little gifts?"

Haydée blanched. Maunsel suspected that she was nervous he would launch into a sarcastic jag that might disclose some indication of anti-Semitism.

But Millie was nothing but gracious: "No, my dear, you simply charge them to your account that's registered on your Band-Aid microchip. You don't actually pay for it. The microchip sends a signal to the master computer system, registers your purchases and the intended recipients. All the info is displayed on that screen above the bandstand. See? Table 47, George Demarest just sent a vial of Absinthe to table 12. The screen also shows what you're drinking, the bar you got it at and a GPS system tracks where you are at the party. It's all up there on the screen for everyone to see. Isn't it fabulous!"

Maunsel looked up at the screen. It looked like the tote board he had seen at the Sports Book at the Bellagio in Las Vegas. He would have to take some time to learn how to read it. He decided to ask another question, if for no other reason than to avoid making eye contact with Shale:

"Why are the microchips embedded in Band-Aids? Is there some significance to that?"

"Well," confided Millie, "someone told me it's there to simulate where you got your morphine injection. It adds to the whole atmosphere of decadence they are going for. You know, de Stijl handled the production of this little party. Outfit out of New York.

They designed the overall interior motif for The Watercress also. They hired actresses to dress up as the various kinds of hookers who walked the streets of Weimar Berlin: fake pregnant '*Munzis*' wearing empathy bellies, 'Gravelstones' with deformities, 'Dominas' in leather boots with whips. Aren't they fabulous?"

At the sound of the word "Watercress," Maunsel was jolted from his daydream. He decided to banish Shale and Millie and Haydée from his immediate thoughts. The Mercedes had reached deep into Jefferson Parish and he had to return his attention to the matter at hand — sexual gratification with Kirsten Duplechain.

As they continued on the interstate out to the Jefferson Parish suburbs, Maunsel took the opportunity to openly survey Kirstin's form. Everything was just right: dark-wash jeans, yellow silk blouse with straining buttons, big hoop earrings, neutral-colored lip gloss, dyed black hair, sandal heels with no stockings, clear fingernail varnish, heavy eyeliner and thick mascara. She also wore some kind of kinetic, motion ring on the middle finger of her right hand with white-gold ringlets that swiveled in orbit around a platinum stud extruding vertically from the ring itself. (He quickly concluded that his wife, Haydée, would never wear such a thing.) She also had a pierced navel, but he couldn't see it. He wondered whether she would consider nipple rings. He decided to launch that campaign later.

"What is Americana?" Maunsel asked. "Sounds like a chain restaurant." He was trying to avoid sounding critical of Metairie restaurants, although he knew he was already being dismissive.

"It's an American fusion place that started in California. They make the best frozen juice drinks there. Fresh squeezed mango and papaya and all kinds of juice. Pineapple. Grapefruit. Whatever you want."

"What is the American cuisine fused *with*?" This question might have sounded sarcastic, but Maunsel really was curious.

"It's a *fusion* restaurant. They have all kinds of flavors. The menu's, like, 10 pages long."

"No, I mean, what kind of cuisine do they fuse

with the American fare?"

"It's a *fusion* restaurant.   They have, like, ginger infused salmon and root beer infused pork chops. The menu's, like, 10 pages long."

Time to bail. "Oh, look! There it is. That's quite a sign they have. Oh, and a drive-thru." He noticed the sign said "Americana!" with an exclamation point — punctuation designed, he presumed, to attract middle-aged singles on the hunt or families looking for a fun outing, or perhaps younger folks on a budget looking to get drunk cheap. On either side of the driveway entrance was a five-foot high twisted helix advertisement sign, Chlorine green on one side and Coast Guard orange on the other that spun in the wind to attract motorists. Maunsel had seen them at used car lots but never at a restaurant. *Oof.*

"We'll only stay a minute. Just to say 'Hi' to Angie and get our drinks. Perfect for the ride to the hotel." She leaned over to kiss him just to remind him, he thought, that she would be making good on more important things later.

After parking the car and making sure she went

through all the unfamiliar steps to kill the engine and shut down all the complicated electronics, Kirstin elevated herself out of the driver's seat, closed the driver side door and waited for Maunsel to do likewise. She pressed the remote control "lock" button on her keychain, whereupon the car issued an electronic "dweep!" and the reverse tail lights blinked twice. Satisfied that the Mercedes was secure in the parking lot, they headed for the restaurant.

Once inside, Maunsel noticed that the air-conditioning system was in fine working order. There was a sweet, roasting aroma to the place and lots of sturdy, dark, polished wood furniture. Kirstin spoke to the 18-year-old hostess wearing a turquoise mini-dress and black Mary Janes with 4 inch heels: "Tell Angie Kirsten's here to see her. We'll be at the bar."

As they approached the bar, Kirstin began taking tiny shuffling steps in feigned excitement that caused her heels to click on the wooden floor: "Jamie! Hi!" she bleated to the linebacker bartender with the orange-colored skin and straw-colored hair. "I'm ready for my papaya!" Maunsel imagined that she had slept with him in the past. Or maybe even in the present. "Jamie this is Maunsel."

"How you doing? What can I get you? One like hers? Here's a list of our specialty drinks if you want to take a gander."

Maunsel surveyed the offerings. At an ordinary bar, he would simply order a beer, but he decided to be a good sport. "I'll try the 'Limonade.' Is that frozen?"

"Oh yeah. One Jugo de Papaya and one Limonade, comin' up." At this point, Angie arrived and she and Kirstin kissed on the cheek. "Hi, Maunsel. Got a hot date this afternoon?" asked Angie, in an insinuating way.

"Hi, Angie. Just picking up a couple of drinks." His response was intended to sidestep Angie's suggestive question. He didn't want to acknowledge to Angie what Angie already knew.

As Angie and Kirstin made small talk, Maunsel busied himself with a quick study of the dinner menu in an attempt to determine exactly what was being fused with what. As it turned out, it was a kind of American-Continental fusion joint. According to the back of the menu, classic American cuisine meets Eurasian fare and a fresh take on Nouvelle American was born! American cuisine, Maunsel learned from the menu, is ideally suited for any type of European, or even Asian, combinant. Maunsel took a look at the list of entrées as blenders whizzed in the background. The descriptions were positively florid:

Roast pork tenderloin with cocoanut turbantoes

House-made hoisin-Seared salmon with crispy sweet potato chips, drizzled cane syrup and honey cous-cous

Costeleta asado, chocolate mole, garlic mashed potatoes

The menu descriptions were obviously composed by menu consultants to sound exotic and daring but the dishes themselves were prepared to accommodate the finicky diner, the unsophisticated palate, the trepidatious culinary sniffler known as the Food Pussy. Many of Maunsel's closest friends were Food Pussies of one sort or another: this one doesn't eat beets and that one doesn't eat anything white. "I'm not really a pastrami guy" one would say or "I'm not a sushi person" or "I don't eat anchovies." Grown men would say these things out loud, even though they were aware that such peevishness would be viewed as infantile or even dainty, but so terrified were they of putting anything more daring than chicken fingers in their mouths that they were willing to suffer the ignominy — men who were never told to eat their peas as children: Food Pussies.

Americana! specialized in the kiddie food that adults could pretend was *haute cuisine*, sickening levels of saltiness or sweetness, all washed down with frozen mojitos or Canadian whiskey and cola. Maunsel couldn't help but feel that the experience was beneath him but the prospect of sex with Kirsten overwhelmed all that was distasteful. He suddenly had a craving for anchovies.

Everything seemed so treacly, like the sauce that came with the sweet and sour pork at the old Cantonese restaurant on Jefferson Highway his parents took him to as a boy. Back then, sweetness meant everything when it came to food. As an adult, he came to prefer anchovies and scotch. But he was in Metairie now with a mistress from Destrehan riding in a white sports car. Jamie handed them their drinks in large Styrofoam cups with lids and straws.

"Thanks, Baby, I'll be back later for dinner," said Kirstin. "Okay, Angie, we gotta go. Ready, Baby?" Maunsel noticed that she called both Jamie and him "Baby." He would have to overlook that coincidence for now.

Back in the car, Maunsel felt it necessary to make some technical inquiries, awkward though they were: "I guess you already have the room key, or room card, whatever it is. We don't need to be showing our faces to the front desk people when we get there. They're going to recognize you right off the bat, anyway. I'd like to get in there as inconspicuously as possible, don't you think?"

"I got it all figured out," said Kirstin. "Shale's got a Tulane Board meeting this afternoon and those go on forever. We can park in a reserved spot in the executive garage, go in the employee entrance, through the kitchen and out into the lobby. We can get on the elevator without even speaking to the front desk people or the bellmen. If anyone asks, you're my brother, Chris, and I'm taking you on an informal tour."

"Okay," said Maunsel, more concerned for her than he was for himself. Nobody in the hotel knew who he was so he wouldn't be the target of informants. "You're the one exposed here, not me. I don't really care." Just then, images of Haydée and Baby Mathilde popped into his head.

"Stop worrying," said Kirstin, in a way, Maunsel thought, designed to take the air out of the conversation. They remained silent for the interstate ride from Metairie to St. Charles Avenue, kept company only by the music of satellite radio tuned to "Hits of the Big 80's." Upon arrival at The Watercress, she guided the car into the executive garage and pulled into a reserved parking spot a short distance from the entrance adjacent to the employee tunnel. An officious looking black man with a perfect mustache, a lime green Nehru tunic and forest green trousers with vertical black stripes on the outside seams approached the driver side door as Kirstin struggled to lift herself out of the low-slung vehicle. "Hello there, Miss Kirstin," he said dutifully.

"Hi, Cedric," she replied. "We won't be long. Just gonna give my brother here a quick tour of the place. Cedric, this is Chris. Chris, Cedric." Maunsel nodded politely. Maunsel wondered whether she had successfully minimized the significance of the event when she said "just gonna give a quick tour." Cedric gave a dubious look.

"I'd ask if you wanted me to get it washed," quipped Cedric, "but I can see it's fresh off the showroom flo'." Maunsel thought he detected something sarcastic in Cedric's tone. He briefly caught Cedric's eye, and quickly looked away, knowing that he looked guilty. As they made their way towards the garage exit, with Kirstin's high heels clicking on the painted concrete pavement, Maunsel turned his head around slightly and saw Cedric reach into the breast pocket of his jacket and pull out a smart phone.

Before he could decide whether he detected anything sinister, Maunsel was being shuffled through a buzzing steel door, past a sunken storeroom where several employees were arguing and where one employee wearing an apron was kneeling in six inches of filthy water. In fact, the whole kitchen seemed to be flooded and the frazzled staff was darting about in an agitated state. Maunsel considered this hectic scene to be an excellent distraction for the stealth operation he and Kirstin were conducting – so distracting, it seemed, that even the front desk clerks and lobby personnel failed to notice as he and Kirstin ducked into an elevator car. As the doors closed, Kirstin nuzzled into his arms and thrust her wet tongue into his mouth. Haydée and Baby Mathilde never entered into his thoughts.

Chapter 8
Dreamcycle

GRETCHEN SOBIESKI PEDALED HER one-speed Huffy Cranbrook Dreamcycle toward downtown on Magazine Street for her field intervention call at the Videau house on Chippewa Street. The knobbed, super fat tires and extra padding on the bicycle seat made for a smooth ride even on the cracked and eroding streets of New Orleans. She took even more delight in her journey because she was falling in love. It was a flush, ebullient feeling because all of the quotidian details of being in relationship were still to come — she could enjoy imagining her immediate future with Jupiter and the places they would be spending time together. Her bike ride that morning was like a romance montage from a 60's movie with sunshine pop tunes performed by The Association or Eternity's Children as the soundtrack. *What rhapsody!* All she needed was a scarf and a wind machine blowing through the jasmine in her mind. Going to work in this state of euphoria was positively delightful. The snail was on the thorn. She was Georgy Girl.

Gretchen let herself slip into a daydream and the memory of first meeting Jupiter at Victor's in the Irish Channel. It was eleven o'clock at night on a Thursday. She sat crossed-legged on a swiveling black vinyl commander's chair at the end of the bar next to the juke box. There were a half-dozen of the regular goofballs killing time arguing and laughing, but the unmatched wooden stool next to her was available. A clean shaven, young black man with medium dreads entered the bar. He walked through the blue smoke and took a seat beside her. *Whoa, daddy . . . this guy is something spectacular.* He looked like one of the Nuba tribesmen photographed by Leni Riefenstahl. He was purity, strength and beauty incarnate. The obsidian monolith spoke to her:

"Hello."

"Maybe," she replied, making sure she smiled to express her receptiveness to flirtation. He got the message.

"Oh, great, I say 'Hello' and you say 'Maybe.' Where do I go from there?"

Gretchen laughed. She would have laughed at anything he said. That kind of thing happens when you are attracted to someone and dropping lots of handkerchiefs. The object of her attraction spoke again.

"Well *you* seem to be happy. Have you and Joe the Bartender been working through the mysteries of the cosmos?"

Gretchen laughed again. She could not have been giving clearer signals. "His name is Frankie." She smiled and then involuntarily ran her fingers through her hair.

"Ah, well then there's one mystery cleared up." The Black Apollo turned to the bartender. "Frankie, may I please have a pint of Bass Ale?"

Gretchen uncrossed her legs and re-crossed

them the other way. She was dancing in her chair. *Maybe if I light a cigarette I will look a little less giddy. I hope he smokes. Say something! Anything!* "You know, if you're thinking about playing something on the juke box, you'll have to wait 'til my selections are finished. Plus, I have complete editorial control over anything you might wanna hear." Gretchen put her hands on her hips in an attitude of mock seriousness and lifted her chin upwards in playful defiance.

"Let me tell you something," he replied, accepting her invitation to flirt. "I listen to the music *I* wanna listen to on *my* terms. I don't generally subject my musical tastes to young ladies with no musical experience who just happen to be sitting closer to the juke box."

Gretchen pretended to stifle her amusement. She felt her eyes brighten. "I'll tell you what. I'll let you make some sample selections, under my supervision, of course, and then decide whether to delete them." She leaned forward slightly in her chair and extended her neck as if to place an impediment to his next move.

"Oh I see," he said. "I gotta pass an audition. Would you like to review my sheet music before I begin?"

Before she knew it, Gretchen and the beautiful black man were bent over the juke box, the old-fashioned kind that had type-written A-side/B-side titles above and below the artists' names and beside alpha-numeric selection codes. As they teased each other about the predictability of their favorites, Gretchen felt the man's arm slip gently around her waist. She moved closer to him so her hip touched his outer thigh. Standing in this position, occasionally shifting her weight from one leg to another, Gretchen sniffed playfully at his musical proposals and scoffed at the explanations he gave in gentle protest. The whole contrapuntal duet was more fun than she had had since her first crush took her to the penny arcade at the Pennsylvania State Fair. From time to time, he would sidle to the bar for another round of foamy, brown beers. The tune selection game would resume and the arm would then return to its place around her waist. Jupiter took the first crack: "Oh, here's one. 'Too Late

to Turn Back Now' by Alex Chilton, live in Belgium."
It was perfect, Jupiter thought. A former 60's pop star
with the band The Box Tops who had a hit with "The
Letter" covering a Cornelius Brothers Sunshine Pop
standard. Chilton, who never recaptured his musical
popularity, had moved to New Orleans in 1982 and
washed dishes at a French Quarter restaurant until his
death in 2010 of a heart attack near his house in Treme.

"I've never heard of that," said Gretchen,
thinking that it sounded like a white group and
wondering whether Jupiter was trying to display racial
diversity in his musical taste. All at once, Gretchen
knew that her competing selection would have great
significance. She wanted to show that she appreciated
all musical genres, especially black ones, but she didn't
want to be cloying. The juke box selection was
extensive, so Gretchen was patient for just the right one
to jump from the display panel. *Aha! Perfect!*

"How 'bout 'Gospel Plow' by Bob Dylan?" she
offered hopefully. It had all the right elements she
wanted to demonstrate to Jupiter: a socially-conscious
folk singer from the 60s covering a classic, southern,

black Baptist gospel hymn with suitable reverence. It had a black association, but it was not patent black pandering.

"Ooh, yeah, that's a good one," said Jupiter. Gretchen got a warm feeling at the thought of Jupiter's approval. The juke box selection game was proving to be a perfect vehicle for a stage-one courtship.

Eventually, Gretchen excused herself to visit the ladies room. She didn't know his name, and he didn't know hers. But it didn't matter. They had been together for two hours and they were both buzzed. *And whispering she would never consent – consented.* When she let him kiss her at the bar some time later, he told her his name was Jupiter and that he was beginning to like the likes of her. Gretchen's memory of this first encounter brought her such happiness that often she would privately smile to herself, even on hot summer mornings when preparing for a professional outreach visit on behalf of Empower the Planet.

And so, it was time to get serious and set her mind to the task at hand. The Videaus were a black family living in the squalor of a federally subsidized apartment with interior drywall breaking off of its studs in waterlogged chunks. She imagined that her arrival on behalf of Empower the Planet would be met with animated appreciation and maybe even a few hugs. *Would that a news crew were here to tape the reception! Such fulfillment! Such chocolate caramel satisfaction!* She would soon be rendering real assistance to real people of need in real moments of urban distress. She would be requisitioning new drywall to repair the rotting mess in the Videau utility room and providing practical advice and education on the ecological value of renewable, sustainable energy efficiency. She had also packed plenty of business cards to distribute to neighbors who might also be desirous of her modest services. *More hugs!*

But the scene outside the Videau home was not what Gretchen expected. There were six or seven black children ranging from ages six to fourteen milling about, but not at play, three of them slowly pedaling mountain bikes in circular or figure "8" patterns, all of them staring at her with what seem to be minatory, and yet still somehow vacant, expressions. From time to time, one of the children would exclaim loudly, but unintelligibly, and two youngsters broke into a fistfight. Gretchen sensed an atmosphere of tension developing. She had seen this before.

She lowered the kickstand on her bicycle, withdrew her purse from the handlebar-mounted basket and smiled at the gathering children. She began to remove the plastic-coated cable that was coiled around the seat shaft, but hesitated. Locking her bike in front of all those forlorn children might be perceived as a gesture of mistrust — racist mistrust. She did not want to be thought of as racist. Besides, these children would not steal a bike from a conscientious girl who was there to render assistance. No, she decided, locking her bike was out of the question.

As Gretchen turned her attention to the Videau residence, she observed a line of three or four adult black men waiting at an open, street-level window. As she walked toward the front door to announce her arrival, the figure of a middle-aged black woman emerged from the window with a paper plate holding a large fillet of fried fish and a scoop of potato salad. The woman in the window handed the plate of food to the first man in line in exchange for several dollar bills.

At the conclusion of two or three of these transactions, Gretchen spoke politely: "Are you Mrs. Videau?"

"Whatchoo want?"

"My name is Gretchen Sobieski. I'm from Empower the Planet, here to take a look at your drywall?"

"Oh, all right." The woman withdrew from the window and opened the front door for the white missionary. "It's in the back. They got sheet rock all over the flo'."

"Excellent," said Gretchen eagerly, as she climbed the steps leading to the interior of the apartment. "I'll just take some measurements and get you all fixed up." Gretchen moved toward the back of the apartment, which, she could not help but notice, smelled heavily of greasy fish frying in oil. She guessed that she might be witnessing some kind of zoning violation involving the sale of prepared food from a private residence. She wondered whether she had an obligation to report any of this or ask to see a permit or something. She put these matters aside for the time being.

Gretchen set her purse down, withdrew her spring activated, retractable tape measure and began taking measurements. At least two full 8 x 4 foot drywall panels had become waterlogged from the busted valve leading to the hot water heater. After taking more measurements, Gretchen took a few steps back to survey the affected area. The damage was not as bad as it looked.

As she turned toward the kitchen to deliver the good news to Ms. Videau, she caught a glimpse of a pre-teen boy reaching into her purse and extracting her smartphone.

"Hey! That's my phone!" Gretchen shouted. Mrs. Videau was back at the window slinging her fish dinners to awaiting men. She had paid no attention to Gretchen up to that point and was similarly oblivious to Gretchen's cries of distress about her smartphone. "Excuse me, Ms. Videau, but your son just swiped my phone from my purse."

"What?" asked Wanda Videau.

"Your son. Or whoever he is, just snatched my cell phone right before my eyes!"

"Vayshawn!" Mrs. Videau called to someone. "Get up in here! Where that lady phone?" Gretchen had noticed that black males under the age of 20 had names with an even number of syllables, either two (Knowshawn, Keyshawn, Marshawn, Tayshawn) or four (Cleanthony, Demariyus, Jadaenean, Barkevius), but that black girls had names with three syllables (Lakeisha, Senesha, Lashondra, Sequoia). None of that made any difference anymore.

Two small boys, approximately aged nine, came bounding up the front steps and into the front of the apartment. Mrs. Videau repeated: "Where dat lady phone?"

The two boys stood motionless as their eyeballs turned in their sockets to observe first, Ms. Videau, then Gretchen, then back to Ms. Videau. "Where dat lady phone?"

The boys spoke meekly: "Ow know."

Gretchen could feel her heart rate begin to

accelerate and her carotid artery throb in her neck. "They're not the ones who took it. It was an older boy. With jeans and a white T-shirt"

"Dey my keeds,"said Ms. Videau, almost completely preoccupied with her food service and with no evident inclination to retrieve Gretchen's stolen smartphone, "Must be somebody else keed." Wanda Videau went back to the open fish window and hollered, "DaVon, get up in here!"

Another boy, approximately age 11, came to the front door. By this time, Gretchen had gathered up her purse, checked to see if any other items had been stolen, and drew the strap over her head so that her purse was in the most secure position possible, with the bag against her left hip and the strap over her right shoulder, one part stretching diagonally down her back and the other diagonally between her breasts and down to the satchel clasp. "That's not him, either. It was an older boy, much taller than him," said Gretchen, her voice fluttering and cracking.

Ms. Videau paid very little attention to Gretchen's protestations and resumed her fried fish food service back at the window. Gretchen shuffled toward the open front door and peered out to the street hoping to spot the perpetrator. But the children had scattered and the only visible people were the men who continued to queue up at the window.

Gretchen pivoted at the threshold and attempted to get Mrs. Videau's attention: "Mrs. Videau, can't you help me? One of those children stole my phone and now he's gone."

"I don't have no phone," said Ms. Videau, her voice beginning to rise and her physical attitude growing more defensive. "Vayshawn don't have no phone. DaVon don't have no phone. You sayin' we took your phone just because we black?"

Gretchen felt an electrical fuzz spread across her scalp. It was the first phase of rage and the second phase of fear. She managed to stifle the urge to lash out at Mrs. Videau for failing to acknowledge the theft and for accusing Gretchen of racism. At that moment Gretchen felt her eyes begin to water. She tried to gather herself together and speak as calmly as possible: "This has nothing to do with black or white, Ms.

Videau. I just need my phone back and I'll be on my way."

"We don't have no phone!" screamed Mrs. Videau in a defiant, righteous tone. "Now getcho fuckin' white ass outta here and go on 'bout yo' business!"

Gretchen could only stand stock still, shaking and clutching her purse. Her brain searched for ideas about how to proceed, but she was paralyzed. Any thoughts she may have had about delivering services to the disenfranchised of New Orleans for their most basic needs had vanished, along with her plans to deliver a tutorial on recycling and energy efficiency. She wanted to proclaim that she had a black boyfriend! She wanted to put up a slide show of her life as a tolerant, sensitive, color blind, Northeastern liberal. But in the end she said nothing.

"I said get the fuck out my house!" shrieked Ms. Videau.

Gretchen spun toward the front door and walked in dejection down the steps and on to Chippewa Street. The only thing she could do was get back on her bike and return to Empower the Planet headquarters to report the incident. But when she lifted her head at the spot where she had parked her bicycle, a scalding gust of panic swept through her – the Dreamcycle had vanished. She looked up towards the window where Mrs. Videau was serving her fish dinners and she could hear herself scream: "Now my bike is gone, too!"

At that very moment, Dennis, Gretchen's supervisor, drew up to the curb in front of the Videau residence in his beat-up Nissan Sentra. Mrs. Videau began screaming obscenities at Gretchen from the window. The men in line for their fish dinners turned away from the window and stared at Gretchen and then at Dennis as he stood in the curb. Children from all over the neighborhood began congregating at the scene. Gretchen involuntarily took two or three shallow breaths that she knew were the beginning of a sobbing breakdown.

"Gretchen! What's going on?" said Dennis in a loud whisper. Gretchen could not, at that moment, respond for fear of bursting into tears. Dennis turned to the open window: "Mrs. Videau! What's going on here?"

"That white bitch up in here talking 'bout we took her cell phone!" said Ms. Videau, assuming for herself the role of accuser.

"Gretchen," said Dennis. "Somebody took your cell phone?"

Gretchen was, by then, visibly weeping, but not sobbing. She tried to pull herself together to answer Dennis' question but still needed more time. Through her tears, she could see that a small throng of black people had gathered in front of the Videau residence, women and children of all ages, on bikes, in strollers, in curlers, in slippers, pushing shopping carts, carrying brickbats, dribbling basketballs, wearing Saints football jerseys, some without shirts at all, everyone contributing to a murmur that was becoming a din. Children squared off for pantomime fistfights and infants shrieked in their mothers' arms. And still the men in line continued to buy the fish dinners Mrs. Videau dispensed through the window.

At last, Gretchen felt composed enough to speak to Dennis: "I was inside taking measurements for the damaged drywall and I saw an older boy reach into my purse and snatch my cell phone. I saw him! He took it! And then he took off down the street!"

Ms. Videau left her post at the service window and descended the steps to present her side of the story to Dennis. "That lady come up in here talking 'bout somebody done stole her cell phone. Don't nobody have no cell phone. Them keeds don't have no cell phone. Go on 'bout your business."

"Dennis! I saw him reach into my purse and take it! I saw him! And when I came outside just to leave, my bike was gone too!" Gretchen had gotten past her tears and was beginning to draw on anger. "Dennis! Tell her to find my cell phone!"

Gretchen could see the gears turning in Dennis' head. She could tell he was more concerned about an escalating racial confrontation that he was about her phone or her bike. She realized Dennis was going to be useless in retrieving her stolen property. It was time for her to consider other options and draw upon alternative resources. What could she do? Jupiter! Jupiter would come to the rescue! He was perfect! He was fearless.

He was black and he loved her.

"Dennis," she spoke assertively, "can I use your phone? I need to call somebody."

"Look, Gretchen. Is your phone really that important? It can be replaced. We'll buy you a new phone and even a new bike. These people don't have anything. Let's just chalk this one up to experience. Let's not get the police involved. Nobody needs all this."

"Just give me your God damn phone, Dennis," Gretchen hissed. *Fuck racial harmony.*

As Dennis reached into his pocket to hand Gretchen his phone, he continued to appeal to her sense of racial magnanimity: "Look, Gretchen, let's just go back to the office and discuss this. You're not going to get your phone back now and there's no point pouring gas on the fire without any chance of resolving the matter." Gretchen was not listening. She was already puzzling out the dial pad on the unfamiliar smartphone.

But, suddenly, Gretchen's heart broke. She did not know Jupiter's telephone number. It was programmed into her smartphone as "Jupiter" and she had never bothered to memorize the actual numbers. She was now completely helpless. Not only could she not contact Jupiter, but Jupiter could not contact her. This was real terror. She could not bear to think of Jupiter trying to reach her unsuccessfully and concluding, not unreasonably, that she wanted to slow things down in their relationship. The corners of her mouth curled downward and her chin trembled. She thrust Dennis' smart phone back into his gut as he continued with his entreaties to her to forget what was "really just an unfortunate misunderstanding." She stalked off Chippewa Street toward her apartment and soon she was into a willing canter. If she could just get to her apartment, she was certain she could find a piece of paper, a matchbook, a business card, something with Jupiter's number on it. If she could be in Jupiter's arms, she wouldn't need a cell phone, a bicycle, Dennis, drywall, justice, racially equality, world peace . . . nothing. She knew then that she wanted nothing but to belong to Jupiter.

Chapter 9

Confrontation at the Watercress

SHALE GIMMEL'S QUICK, SCAMPERING exit from the Tulane Board of Governors meeting meant that he never heard the resolution of the "New Student Orientation" controversy or the Board's decision on how to respond to the demands of the Asian-American Students Union. The aborted cafeteria *tête-à-tête* with Pocahontas Melville vanished from his thoughts. The text message from his hotel garage manager directed Shale's attention exclusively to the arrival of his mistress and her suspected paramour at The Watercress. *At my own hotel! In my reserved parking space!* Kiddo's impatient departure earlier that morning from Monaco Motor Cars in the white Mercedes-Benz C250 Coupe he bought for her *(leased)* had made him suspicious at the time, but it did not register as a full-fledged warning sign. He felt like a cuckold. Exactly why he felt betrayed when he himself was committing adultery he could not say, but a prickly rage flowed through him nevertheless.

By the time Shale reached the main exit of the Lavin-Bernick Student Center, he had removed his suit jacket and folded it over his left arm, anticipating that the long walk/run to his car parked on the other side of Willow Street in the September heat would cause him to perspire a great deal, even if he made his way there in shirt sleeves. Ordinarily, an upcoming meeting with Kiddo would involve a preliminary checklist of hygienic touchups (chewing breath mints, trimming nose hairs, combing-over his regular hair, applying light makeup, *etc.*), but, for this mission, he was going commando.

Before he was even in sight of his silver Cadillac XTS sedan, he repeatedly pressed the "unlock" button on his remote control keychain thinking that it would save him even as much as three seconds in his scramble to get his departure underway. He let the beeping sounds of the automobile's "unlock" notification system be his guide. He arrived at the driver side at last and pulled the door handle. As the door opened, a blast of heat rose up to his face from the inside of the car where a combination of tropical sun, closed windows and black leather upholstery had created a hotbox. The back of his legs were singed when he took his place in the driver's seat and the steering wheel burned his hands. But he had no time to be irritated. The engine started willingly and he guided the Cadillac out of the parking lot on to Willow Street and then over to Freret Street, which ran parallel to St. Charles Avenue, whence The Watercress, some thirty blocks away.

Along the way Shale passed Alcée Fortier Senior High School (public) where most of his childhood friends from the Dryades Street neighborhood had attended (the Shapiro boys, Julius Orlansky, Adam Rosenblat, and the rest of his lower-middle class *Ostjuden* running mates). By the time

Shale had reached high school age, his parents had migrated to Lakewood South and could afford to send him to Isidore Newman School, the private and more expensive college preparatory institution that had its start at the turn of the century as a trade school for Jewish orphans. It was founded by the distinguished German-Jewish philanthropist who made his fortune financing Southern railroads but was most known as the principal investor in the Maison Blanche department store on Canal Street. By the time he was a senior, Shale was happy enough to be enrolled at Newman. As a freshman, though, he longed to attend public school Fortier High, which was more blue-collar, with a little bit tougher group of boys and a less presumptive Jewish association than Isidore Newman. When the time came for his father to decide where Shale would attend high school, his family no longer lived in the district from which Fortier drew, and the increasing infusion of black students as a consequence of desegregation made the choice an easy one. None of this mattered anymore because, after Hurricane Katrina, Fortier ceased operations as a public high school under the administration of the Orleans Parish School Board, only to resume as a magnet school chartered by the state-run Recovery School District under the supervision of Tulane University. He glanced at the four story Italian Renaissance edifice as he sped down Freret Street and noted that the physical plant looked smarter and more well-kept than it ever had before.

But this nostalgia was a distraction from Shale's immediate mission. He therefore stiffened himself in the driver seat and proceeded down Freret Street. When he reached the stoplight at Louisiana Avenue, he was again distracted by another landmark of his youth. At that corner was a vacant lot where the Original Brown Derby Lounge and Package Liquor Store once stood. Just exactly why this Brown Derby was the *original* Brown Derby, presumptively predating the one in Los Angeles, Shale could not say. As an undergraduate at Tulane, he made many trips to that celebrated black establishment to pick up inebriated members of the rhythm-and-blues band his fraternity would hire to perform at Saturday night parties. In those days, the Original Brown Derby was a rough joint, but it posed no real threat to college boys calling to collect wayward or forgetful musicians occasionally retained for the amusement of Newcomb College co-eds. Shale was a member of Sigma Alpha Mu, or "Sammy" as it was then known, the less prestigious Jewish fraternity, one step down from Zeta Beta Tau, the first string Jewish House, that would not have him. *Ostjuden* were excluded by fancy Jews even at the college level. Monuments to his caste resentment were around every corner. The Brown Derby burned down shortly after Hurricane Katrina and there remained no trace of its ramshackle mystique. Shale looked upon the vacant parcel and despaired.

When the light turned green, Shale made the dog-leg left onto La Salle Street in the shadow of the old Flint-Goodrich Hospital designed by the legendary Moise Goldstein and continued through Central City as La Salle turned into Simon Bolivar Avenue. Now he could see the high-rise office buildings of the Central Business District in the distance and he became aware that he needed to turn right to get to St. Charles Avenue.

He did so on Felicity Street and found himself in the center of his old Dryades Street neighborhood now almost exclusively black. In truth, the neighborhood was more than half abandoned, dotted by truck marshalling yards, shabby bodegas and salvage shops. Distress and desuetude as far as the eye could see. Almost nothing was left of the once bustling Orthodox Jewish sector of his youth. It was empty but evident: the JoAnn Shop for girls, Kaufman's department store, Rosenblat's butcher shop and the gigantic, imposing nucleus of the community, Congregation Beth Israel. Shale was always careful to recall that it was "Congregation" Beth Israel not "Temple" Beth Israel, a term used as a replacement for "synagogue" by Reform Jews bent on assimilation-at-any-cost, embarrassed as they were of their Eastern European brethren who refused to stifle their ethnic ways of life for the good of overall Jewish acceptance. *(Oh, to FIT IN!)* On top of his feelings of personal jealousy of his promiscuous mistress, Shale felt the familiar creep of cultural resentment — quite an emotional state for a 64-year-old man headed for an unpredictable and surely volatile confrontation.

Shale blew through the old neighborhood, barreled on to St. Charles Avenue and turned sharply on Josephine Street where he would enter The Watercress parking garage behind the hotel. He nosed his Cadillac into the first available parking spot and shut off the engine. As he looked out of the driver side window, he saw Cedric scurrying over to greet him. Shale instinctively took an inventory of Cedric's uniform as he always did, conditioned, as he was, by the de Stijl designers to monitor whether his employees were upholding the aesthetic policy that was essential to the overall thematic palette and decorative motif.

"Mr. Shale! You got here quick! They went in through the employee entrance about 20 minutes ago," said Cedric, imparting as much information as he could under the circumstances. Shale was already marching hard toward the employee entrance. Shale had abandoned his suit coat in the car and had only one question for Cedric hustling behind him: "Who is she with?"

"She said it was her brother," Cedric responded.

"I don't know. They didn't look alike. They was inside the hotel 'fo I could figure anything out."

"Take my car and block that white Mercedes," said Shale, tossing the car keys to Cedric. He was, for an instant, distracted by what he thought was the scent of a familiar department store perfume. "Nobody leaves this garage unless I say so."

"Copy that," said Cedric, who seemed delighted to be part of the spontaneous private police action. And yet, Shale thought he heard Cedric snicker.

No matter. Shale walked menacingly up the cement incline of the employee entrance tunnel, breathing heavily from adrenaline, not fatigue. When he reached the shipping and receiving clerk window he barked: "Open the Godddamn door!"

The clerk buzzed him through and Shale was immediately struck by the sight of a flooded kitchen. His *maître d'*, Fabrizio, was standing with his hands on his hips near the threshold of a sunken storeroom flooded with six inches of water. Fabrizio was speaking excitedly with a light-skinned black man, some kind of kitchen manager, who obviously wanted to say something but was holding back. The rest of the kitchen staff was mopping or cleaning or stacking or storing, all with their heads down. Puzzled at the scene, but still focused, Shale sloshed past Fabrizio and the light-skinned black man and headed for the lobby. His supervisory instinct prompted him to consider a reprimand for the use of expensive Italian linens to soak up filthy bilge water, but he let it go. Fabrizio caught sight of him and exclaimed, "Mr. Gimmel! We're mopping up much wadder! Please watch your trousers!"

"Just clean up this disaster," said Shale, barely acknowledging Fabrizio's existence, and completely ignoring the existence of the light-skinned black man. Shale pushed through the swamp. After a few wet strides, Shale was in the hotel lobby. It was carpeted in a sumptuous green pile and embroidered with custom-made blue floriform designs. Curvilinear *Art Nouveau* organics dripped everywhere.

Shale was a waterlogged *zhluhb* by the time he pressed his torso against the green marble front desk ramparts. He said to the perfectly appointed female

Vietnamese clerk: "Give me a master pass key." He had no intention of explaining the urgency of his visit or otherwise letting on what he was up to. For the first time, he noticed his own heavy breathing, so he swallowed to try and make it stop. He also sensed that a bead of perspiration was dangling from the tip of his nose. Demon Embarrassment had decided to appear in the *mise-en-scene*, reminding Shale of the origins of an unfortunate sexual episode still fresh in his memory, and it occurred to him that his base makeup might be clumping. He wiped the tip of his nose with the cuff of his sleeve. *What would the little oriental sexpot think of this disgusting presentation?*

The extraordinarily beautiful girl knew exactly who Shale was. Silently, nervously, but with purpose, she placed a light green, plastic, computer-encoded access key, the size and shape of a credit card, into a blinking, black, specially magnetized cradle and programmed it as a master. Within thirty seconds, the master key-card was in the damp hand of her obviously distressed boss.

Master key-card in hand, Shale squished a few

steps towards the elevator doors and pressed the heat-sensitive "up" button, which was also dimpled in Braille. In no time, he heard an elevator chime, and the door to one of the three shafts opened. He boarded and pressed "M" for mezzanine and thought to himself: "She's either in the Celeriac Suite or the Verdigris Suite. That little trashbag is going to regret this." Alone in the elevator, he searched for a reflecting surface to evaluate his appearance. The walls were tufted upholstery, but the button panel was chrome-plated and provided a sharp, somewhat distorted image of his mottled countenance. Resigned to the futility of constantly maintaining his outward appearance, he stared blankly at the precise point where the vertical seam of the two elevator doors met the metal lintel. He exhaled.

The Celeriac Suite appeared directly opposite the elevator door. Shale rubbed the master key card against the matte black rectangular sensor beneath the door handle. A green light began to blink on the silver bracket that housed the sensor and he pushed open the door. At first he thought he had selected the wrong room as nothing inside of the suite appeared to be out of place, at least nothing in the sitting room that was separated from the bedroom by open double, swinging doors. As he made his way farther into the suite, he heard some unintelligible chit chat between a man and a woman coming from the bedroom. *Could this be them? Or did I just barge in on an innocent couple paying $2500 a night?*

Nope. It was Kiddo and her boyfriend. *Haven't I seen this guy somewhere before?* The darling lovebirds wriggled under the white sheets and groped for the green-on-green, striped duvet. Her dark hair contrasted beautifully with the white pillow case. The boyfriend's head sank lower and lower into the bedding and almost disappeared. It reminded Shale of the way Bartholomew Dolliole would dissolve under the conference room table whenever a Tulane Board of Governors meeting took up a touchy political issue. Still, there was nowhere for the boyfriend to go. *This guy looks very familiar to me.*

"Shale!" she cried. "What the fuck?"

Shale entered the bedroom and took a seat on a

Eugene Guillard chair upholstered in teal green mohair. The luminists at de Stijl had spared no expense furnishing the luxury suites at The Watercress. "Well," he began, with a twisted grin. "How are y'all doing?"

Chapter 10
Bullpup

JUPITER MINGO STOOD TENNIS-SHOE deep in the Watercress kitchen and burned. The Watercress kitchen was flooded and Josephine Boniface was dead. Brandon Cazenave and Fabrizio Mariposa would soon be dead. Gretchen Sobieski was not responding to his text messages. Jupiter was feeling the universe collapse around him. His ears felt like they were on fire and yet it was time to take action. Jupiter would reach his locker in the employee dressing room adjacent to the shipping and receiving office in only a few strides from the flooded storeroom. As he approached, he removed his waterlogged apron and tossed it on the cement floor. He carefully dialed in the combination on his padlock and took an inventory of his remaining garments: soaking wet high top tennis shoes (tightly laced), black and white checked gingham dishwasher's pants (also soaking wet) and a white T-shirt. His smartphone was in his pants pocket but he was unsure whether water had compromised its operability since the last time he checked, but he had not heard any notification tones.

The padlock on his locker snapped open with a downward tug and Jupiter slipped the U-bolt from the eye of the latch mechanism and lifted the chrome-plated sliding part of the metal fixture upwards about one inch on its travel rail. The long, rectangular locker door popped open and shivered on its hinges. As he bent down to unzip the main pouch of his nylon backpack, Jupiter noticed that his hands were not shaking. He reached into the main pouch and retrieved his Herstal P90 fully-ambidextrous Bullpup submachine gun, propped the rubber butt of the weapon against his left thigh and set its muzzle against the inside wall of his locker. He then re-zipped the backpack's main pouch so that it was completely closed and the remaining contents were secure. Next, he unzipped an auxiliary side pouch and reached in to remove one of the 50-round detachable magazines he had packed earlier that morning. Proceeding methodically, Jupiter clipped the magazine on the topside of the Bullpup and set the firing option selector switch to "burst" so that each trigger squeeze would discharge only three 5.7 mm bullets at a time. He reached into his pants pocket for what seemed like the one-hundredth time hoping for a message from Gretchen. Finding none, he re-sent his last message to her. At that very moment, he heard Brandon Cazenave, who had followed him into the dressing area, say: "What the fuck, Jupiter? Get back in the kitchen."

Keeping his gaze fixed downward, Jupiter smiled to himself and slipped his arms through the padded shoulder straps of his backpack as he switched the Bull pup from one hand to the other. Now tight as a tick and gathered for battle, Jupiter spun around toward Brandon and shouldered his weapon in combat firing position. He spoke softly in a Creole *patois* that, in what was to be the last of the day's ironies, Brandon would not understand: *"Cancrelat sourti dans lafarine."*

"What the fuck?" said Brandon looking baffled by the sight of a dark-skinned dishwasher brandishing a fierce looking firearm. Jupiter enjoyed stumping Brandon with obscure demotic French expressions.

But back to business. Jupiter activated the red laser aiming beam and whispered: *"Carbon zames va done la farine."*

"Huh?" Brandon grunted in a suddenly far less imperious way. He was, after all, staring down the barrel of an automatic assault rifle.

"You don't even understand your own fucking Boscoville language," said Jupiter with his lips mashed against the butt of the Bullpup and his left eye closed. Jupiter squeezed the trigger once and only once, whereupon three short pulse-blasts issued from the flaming muzzle of the weapon and three bronze shell casings sprang from the underside discharge window of the breach. The bullets pierced Brandon's sternum and bright red blood spurted from his chest as he collapsed almost gently to the cement floor. Jupiter lowered the weapon to waist level and noted the smell of smoke and the sound of silence. Brandon was dead.

Jupiter proceeded into the kitchen and advanced on his next target. Fabrizio Mariposa stood before a group of three black busboys berating them for reasons Jupiter could not ascertain. They were the same boys Jupiter had seen Fabrizio mysteriously slipping cash to from time to time. Fabrizio had his back to Jupiter, but the busboys where facing him as he approached the small group suffering the upbraid. Jupiter noticed one of the busboys swallow hard.

"What are joo looking at?" screamed Fabrizio at the busboys who were no longer paying attention to the incensed Mexican. At that point, Fabrizio turned to face Jupiter who was holding what must, to Fabrizio, have looked like a super-soaker squirt gun. Jupiter circled around Fabrizio so that the busboys were no longer in his line of fire. This time, Jupiter had nothing to say. He squeezed the trigger of the Bullpup once, and only once, discharging another volley of three pulse-bursts into Fabrizio's face. There was another puff of smoke and the sound of shell casings hitting the tile floor. Fabrizio's slim corpse crumpled to the floor. This time, there really was silence in the kitchen. The frightened busboys stared at Jupiter.

"Relax," said Jupiter. "You boys are cool." But the next character to appear on the scene was not. The shrimp cocktail beat cop had heard the report and slipped into the kitchen from his sentry post in the lobby. He had drawn down his service pistol and was assessing matters in what to Jupiter looked like police academy combat position. But Jupiter saw him first and fired a quick pulse-burst. This time, his victim was lifted off his feet. The policeman's service pistol flew toward the kitchen hot line and he landed on his back, eyes open, still breathing heavily. Jupiter walked closer and stood over the terrified cop. Jupiter could not make out what he was trying to say – was he asking for mercy? Muttering curse words in defiance? It didn't make any difference to Jupiter. He thrust the muzzle of the Bullpup into the cop's gasping, foamy mouth and pulled the trigger. Jupiter was beginning to loosen up.

Things were proceeding nicely, thought Jupiter,

as he splashed through the kitchen and into the hotel lobby as the staff stood motionless and stared. But the temporary sense of satisfaction departed when he remembered that Miss Josephine lay dead at the hands of the New Orleans Police Department. They would be coming for him soon. It seemed to him like a good time to go check out some of the luxury suites in the hotel where he might find a rich quarry of white folks at their dissipated leisure. He was, at that point, so deep in blood that sin began to pluck on sin.

From the kitchen, Jupiter walked into and through the lobby, passing the front desk clerks on his way to the first floor elevator access area. The beautiful Vietnamese girls gave off an ultra-violet brilliance as they stood behind the front desk with their hair pulled back into tight buns, motionless and silent and elegant as the pottery that adorned practically every horizontal surface in the lobby's receiving area. There was no need for Jupiter to press the call button for an elevator because one car was waiting, retractable doors already open.

Jupiter boarded calmly, with his Bullpup at

waist level, and pressed "M" on the floor selection panel. During his short trip up only one story, he noticed the first signs of perspiration and tingling nerves. He knew that when the elevator door opened, there would be violence. He checked the action on his instrument and confirmed that the firing selection mechanism was still set to "burst." He thought about Gretchen. *Why won't she text me?* He heard the elevator chime and saw the doors glide open.

As he got off, Jupiter heard a commotion from the Celeriac Suite immediately opposite the elevator. There was a young, naked white man, who looked to be approximately 35 years old, walking briskly out of the hotel room holding a plump, green silk sofa cushion over his crotch with one hand and an identical cushion over the crack of his ass with the other. The man seemed to be in some distress and Jupiter heard the voice of a woman screaming "Wait, Maunsel, wait!"

From inside the suite, Jupiter heard an older man's voice shouting "Maunsel? I thought his name was Chris?"

The young white man with the sofa cushion

loincloth started towards Jupiter in an attempt to catch the elevator before the door closed. "Watch out, dude," said the frantic refugee. Jupiter didn't like the tone of the man's voice even though he found it somewhat humorous. White people disporting throughout luxury hotels with no clothes on, while decidedly zany in a burlesque kind of way, disgusted Jupiter. That image quickly metamorphosed into a threatening convolusion of barbed wire and stainless steel rock-a-chaws. One squeeze of the Bullpulp while still at waist level let fly another burst of ordnance. This time a cloud of feathers flew into the smoke-filled air before the next bag of bones pitched to the carpeted floor. Only then did Jupiter see blood ooze from the lifeless corpse.

With his next victim dispatched, Jupiter looked up at the doorway leading into the suite and beheld a naked woman with obvious breast implants running towards the body of her dead lover. Without even noticing Jupiter, the hysterical bombshell knelt before the bloody and befeathered body of the white boy. Sobbing and crying and holding his dead head in her hands, she turned back toward the suite and screamed,

"You didn't have to shoot him!"

Just then, a disheveled older Jewish-looking man with tiny red capillaries bursting on the surface of his cheeks and nose took one step into the hallway and said, "I didn't shoot him! I would have! But I didn't!"

"Excuse me, Miss," interrupted Jupiter. "He didn't shoot him. I did." The puzzled ecdysiast looked up at Jupiter from her crouching position and managed to mumble, "Huh?" as she tried to take stock of the chaos. Jupiter squeezed the trigger of his Bullpup yet again and three steel bullets entered the crown of her head, cracking her skull and causing bits of brain matter to splash on the reddened cheeks of the wizened old man standing in the doorway. Suddenly, as if he understood the real urgency of the situation, the older man with brains all over his translucent face retreated into the hotel suite and tried to shut the entrance door. Jupiter fired another burst into the closing door. Splinters of green lacquered wood exploded into the hallway and the spring-loaded door failed to shut completely.

Jupiter moved toward the damaged door and

gently pushed it open. The older man was lying on his back just inside the hallway holding his belly as blood seeped from between his fingers. Jupiter immediately concluded that his aged victim was merely wounded, not dead. The man, in obvious agony, tried to speak: "Wait. Wait. I can give you money."

"Shut the fuck up, Goldberg." Jupiter wondered where this anti-Semitic remark came from but he meant for it to eliminate any interruption to his methodical undertaking.

"The name's Gimmelfarb."

Jupiter froze in his tracks. The old man said something that sounded decidedly familiar. He inquired: "What did you say?"

"I said, 'My name's Gimmelfarb.'"

Jupiter knew that name somehow. *Wasn't the name of the hotel's owner, Gimmelfarb, or something like that? Do I have the owner of The Watercress in my crosshairs?* Jupiter continued his inquiry: "What kind of fucking name is that?"

"It's Polish. Or maybe Lithuanian. I'm a Polish Jew. I grew up on Dryades Street, right around the corner from here."

Jupiter immediately recognized the psychological technique the man was trying to deploy: The hostage must humanize himself in the eyes of the hostage-taker. Jupiter relaxed slightly and spoke: "And just what, exactly, is that supposed to get you?"

"Maybe it gets me my life back," said Old Gimmelfarb, on his back breathing heavily and wiping clumps of what seemed to be flesh-colored makeup off his splotchy face. "Maybe it gets me my life back."

Jupiter saw a look of resignation inhabit the old man's face as he turned on his hip and braced himself with his arms on the luxurious celadon-colored carpeting of the hotel room floor. Jupiter took his finger off the trigger of the Bullpup and let it descend to hip level. The old man had lost his expression of terror and seemed to be reflecting upon something other than the immediate exigency. For some reason, Jupiter decided that Old Gimmelfarb of Dryades Street would be spared. But Jupiter could not linger. It was time to flee the hotel premises and find a more secure redoubt in the surrounding neighborhood.

Before his departure, Jupiter thought to create a distraction for the swarms of law enforcement personnel that were surely headed for The Watercress. So he aimed his weapon at the door handle of a suite adjacent to the one where Gimmelfarb lay and fired another burst. The door swung open, and Jupiter entered to find it vacant. He snatched a mint colored aluminum wastepaper basket from under an antique work desk in the outer room of the suite. He filled it with sheets of lime green stationery, copies of several luxury shelter magazines and several handfuls of facial tissue. He placed the wastepaper basket under one of the windows with a view onto St. Charles Avenue. He deposited the bottom end of an emerald-green brocade curtain into the mouth of the container. He then reached into the auxiliary pouch of his backpack, removed a cigarette lighter and lit the contents of the wastepaper basket on fire. Almost immediately, the drapery was aflame as well.

At this stage of his measured rampage, he had to move quickly. And yet, his hallucinations were growing more and more intense. A gathering of crustaceous crypto-glyphs scampered across the surface of his very vulnerable imagination. He remembered his Chaucer and the concept of *corages*: A medieval admixture of valor, heart and lust (both sanguinary and sexual). Jupiter found himself driven by sharp pangs of vengeance and a chivalric motivation to demonstrate to Gretchen his worthiness, whether she ever knew about it or not.

Instead of waiting for an elevator, Jupiter went to the emergency stairs and descended to the first floor. He emerged into the lobby with the Bullpup at his waist and sprinted for the front door facing St. Charles Avenue. Before he could reach it, he was forced to stop abruptly – through the glass doors, he could see three white policemen in sky blue shirts and navy blue trousers with pistols drawn heading into the hotel lobby area. Their body profiles were decidedly more angular than the squishy policemen he was accustomed to encounter throughout the day. The contrast between the sky blue and navy blue of their uniforms seemed to Jupiter the concentrated flame that forms at the tip of an acetylene blowtorch. He quickly reset the firing selection mechanism from "burst" to "fully automatic."

As the three officers came through the glass doors of the hotel, Jupiter sprayed a barrage of steel at the oncoming enemy. All three dropped dead. With the weapon fully automated, it generated quite a bit more smoke than it had with previous discharges. The report was much louder, causing Jupiter's ears to ring. The front desk clerks, the bellmen and the various concierge staff members must have taken cover because there were no humans in sight, save for the three dead police officers. Jupiter concluded that those three were not alone and that the hotel was probably surrounded. The only option he had was to head for the roof of the hotel and attempt to jump to an adjacent building, if there was one and if such a traversion was possible. The best way up, he concluded, was the employee elevator that was accessible from the ground floor near the employee locker room.

To get to the employee elevator from the lobby, Jupiter had to go back through the kitchen, which was deserted and still flooded from the broken dishwasher pipe. He passed the recessed storeroom (also still flooded) and the office of the shipping and receiving clerk (also empty). He boarded the employee elevator and began his ride up to the 13th floor. *En route*, Jupiter was able to set down his weapon and retrieve a bottle of water from his backpack. He guzzled half of it, returned the bottle to the main pouch and zipped it back up. He checked his smartphone for any word from Gretchen, but there was none. *Why did I buy those blue pajamas?* He thrust the device back into his pants pocket out of habit.

When he reached the 13th floor, he trotted down a narrow, low-ceilinged hallway at the end of which was the door to the hotel wine storage room. The door was not locked, so he entered and proceeded between the racks and racks of wine bottles towards another door that he knew led to the exterior rooftop. Halfway there, he returned to the interior door of the wine room and placed a bottle of wine on the top edge of the door panel that he set slightly ajar. That way, if the police were to enter in search of him, the wine bottle would fall and crash on the floor — a kind of makeshift tocsin against any ambuscade.

This was as much preparation as he could put in place. So he proceeded to the exterior door of the wine room and walked onto the hotel roof, which was, essentially, the ceiling of the 12th floor. He walked to the edge of the roof on the St. Charles Avenue side of the building, with roof gravel crunching under each step. There was a two foot brick retaining edge that circumscribed the entire exposed roof level and offered some measure of safety from fall, but it had probably been designed by Messrs. Weiss and Dreyfous for decorative purposes only. As Jupiter peered over that low barrier, he could see a hook-and-ladder company of the fire brigade already taking positions to put out the fire he had started on the mezzanine level. It appeared to Jupiter that St. Charles Avenue had been blocked off to vehicular traffic from Jackson Avenue to St. Andrew Street. An armored SWAT vehicle was rolling slowly along the neutral ground where the streetcar tracks were laid. Dozens of police cars with flashing white strobe lights were parked willy-nilly on the streets below and Jupiter could see that several police officers were crouching behind those vehicles for cover with semi-automatic pistols drawn. Some even had shotguns trained at the front door the hotel. So far as he could tell, the police were completely unaware that he had taken refuge on the roof.

Jupiter dropped to a crouch. He checked his smartphone for what he guessed might be the last time — nothing. As he despaired, he drank the rest of the water from his plastic bottle. When he finished, he crept softly around the exposed area of the roof and found that there were no neighboring buildings that he could possibly jump to and make his escape. The Avenue Hotel stood directly across Josephine Street but was actually taller than The Watercress. Jupiter realized that police snipers could and would probably take position there if his own position on the roof of The Watercress was ever discovered.

The endgame of this firefight began to dawn on him. The roof of The Watercress was where he would die. At some point, he would have to give up his whereabouts, take with him as many cops as he could and commit suicide. Of one thing he was sure: the scorecard of death would reckon in his favor by the time he was through. He would have to initiate a final showdown with policemen on foot attempting a rooftop assault.

But that was not going to happen until the authorities were aware that he was actually *on* the roof. To begin the *Gotterdammerung*, Jupiter would have to reveal his position by firing upon the besiegers. "I might as well get started," he thought to himself. So he checked to see that the action on his Bullpup was clear and that he did not need a fresh magazine of ammunition. He flipped the firing selection switch back to "burst." He stood up from his seated position and crept to the edge of the roof facing St. Charles Avenue. As he peered down, he could see that a fireman with a canvas hose over his shoulder and a brass nozzle in his clutches was ascending a telescoping truck ladder to extinguish the blaze flaming out of a lower hotel window. Jupiter drew a bead on the faceless, dehumanized fireman and squeezed off a triple burst. At least one bullet struck the firefighter in his hand but the other two missed completely. The brave man dropped the hose but was able to cling to the ladder and begin an emergency descent. At that point, every cop in the contingent began firing whatever weapon he happened to be brandishing and larger caliber rounds whizzed up towards the roof from specially armed forces on the ground.

That would soon change. Once fire from the ground died down, Jupiter could hear the unmistakable sound of a helicopter making its way toward The Watercress. Almost simultaneously, Jupiter heard the crashing sound of his wine bottle alarm from inside the wine cellar. He switched his firing mechanism to "fully automatic" and opened the exterior door that led from the wine cellar to the rooftop. He was met immediately by the sight of no fewer than seven police officers headed in his direction. This detachment flashed across his mind's eye like the saber-toothed wheels of a metal crushing machine at a scrap recycling yard. Jupiter unloaded the remainder of his magazine against the on-rushers and dropped them one and all, their blood mixed with rivers of red wine and broken glass from bottles busted by his indiscriminate firing. The threat was not entirely eliminated. There was another police detachment that had not yet ventured into the wine room killing zone. Jupiter could hear a reserve platoon screaming and barking orders and making ready for a second assault. Jupiter had no choice but to retreat to the exposed area of the roof, but that meant he would take fire from the helicopter, if indeed it was armed.

Sure enough, the roof gravel around his feet exploded with heavy caliber gunfire from above. Jupiter was able to find a small concrete enclave that had a half-roof and three walls. Each time the helicopter circled overhead to fire at the enclave on its un-walled side, Jupiter was able to grasp a horizontal water pipe or electrical conduit high in the interior of the enclave, lift his legs to his chest as if doing schoolyard calisthenics and avoid the bullets coming from the helicopter rifleman. After two or three passes, the helicopter mysteriously pulled back and flew away towards the Superdome farther downtown. Perhaps, thought Jupiter, they were out of fuel or ammunition or both. No matter. The disappearance of the helicopter allowed Jupiter to get his feet on the roof once more and prepare for an expected charge from the second wave of wine room infantry.

Although it was getting past 5:00 PM, there was still plenty of daylight. Jupiter scanned the roof for a strategic hiding spot to wage the next stage of this war. Diagonally across the roof from the concrete enclave were two large metal structures that apparently housed machinery (compressors or generators or condensers) associated with the industrial air-conditioning system. Bullpup in his hand and backpack on his back, Jupiter scrambled across the gravel roof and pried open one side of the sheet metal casing. With some effort, he was able to bend back the sheet metal and squeeze inside. This position served as an excellent hiding spot but it completely prevented him from delivering return fire should he be discovered. Out of the crucible, into the brazier. But, it would have to do.

He detached the empty magazine of his Bullpup, slapped in a fresh clip and thought about Robert Charles and the homemade bullets he used to fight off a similar police assault over 100 years before. Robert Charles was killed when the police set fire to his weatherboard bunker and flushed him out. That was not going to happen to Jupiter.

As he rested, Jupiter could feel his adrenaline level drop and his energy drain. Soon he began to feel a burning, excruciating pain in his left thigh and left hip. He placed his fingers on the affected areas, raised them to his face and saw and smelled blood. He was hit. He checked his smartphone one last time. Futility. Instead of returning the device to his pocket he tossed it onto the roof of the hotel. Suddenly, he heard clattering and shouting from the door of the wine room followed by the footfall of police boots on gravel.

"There's blood flowing from that H-VAC unit!" he heard a voice say. "He's hiding in the unit! He's hiding in the unit!"

Jupiter's cover was blown. Instinctively, he reached for the Bullpup and attempted to position himself for a counter attack. The close quarters made things difficult. The Bullpup slipped from his bloody hands and clanked against the sheet metal casing. Jupiter was helpless.

The police moved in. "He's making a move! Take cover and fire on my command!" It was the last thing Jupiter Mingo heard.

Epilogue

Epilogue

SHALE GIMMELFARB, HIS FLESH wounds bandaged with heavy gauze, sat at a table in the hotel restaurant of The Watercress along with a passel of police lieutenants, FBI agents (holsters strapped to their thighs by nylon garters) and assorted officers from United States Department of Homeland Security. They were all white and they all had mustaches. By the time the group had assembled at 8 PM, the war was over. One black man lay dead on the roof of the hotel. The bodies of an Hispanic male, a light-skinned black male and two white civilians had been packed in body bags and sent on their way to the coroner for postmortem examinations. Eleven police officers were dead including poor Officer Danny Connelly who had the misfortune of taking a private detail on the only day that hotel security would ever be threatened. Shale, himself, was exhausted but peaceful. He wondered why his bullet wounds were causing him no pain.

Captain Salvatore Giambelluca sipped black coffee from a demitasse with a green "M" glazed on the outer porcelain. A black Herstal P90 Bullpup automatic assault rifle lay clear at the center of a mint green tablecloth-covered table. Captain Giambelluca had managed to survive the mêlée. He explained to Shale that he had been part of the rooftop assault force and even delivered the kill shot through the air conditioning fan's metal housing. Had there been an additional gunman, as they initially suspected, the Captain may not have made it. He never asked Shale how he had managed to survive, even though he had been face-to-face with the killer longer than anyone.

Giambelluca spoke: "Arright. There's no one else. He was by himself. Right? Everything's been searched and secured? I've gotta tell the mayor something for the press conference. They already reported a copy-cat sniper at the Plaza Tower. We gotta deal with the Harlem Globetrotters playing at the downtown arena tonight. Mayor wants to know whether to cancel the show. Plus we got the regular shit in the Quarter to deal with. The Chief is on his way too. Is there someone from Homeland Security gonna read a statement? There's no Muslim component to any of this, is there?"

Special Agent Fed #1: "No. No. We're searching Mingo's apartment now. There's almost nothing in there. No computer. No Arabic literature. Just a lot of old history books and novels. A complete set of the Oxford English Dictionary. Nothing about Al Qaeda or Hezbollah. Nothing. His backpack had a book about a riot in New Orleans in 1900. Somebody named Robert Charles killed a bunch of police officers. Sounds more like suicide by cop."

FBI Profiler: "We've uncovered no possible source of despondence. But he's been a dishwasher here at The Watercress for the past several years. Looks like he may have had a beef with his kitchen supervisors. At this point, he's a bit of a mystery but we've uncovered no larger cause or *jihad* of any kind. We're checking his texts and cell calls now. It looks like he'd been trying to reach a girl named 'Gretchen' right up until the end. They had spoken earlier today. Call lasted about two minutes. He tried to text her a dozen times after that but she never responded. We're trying to trace the phone number now. We don't know who she is."

Shale hardly noticed the dutiful forensic activity swirling around him. Local and national media were on the scene mixed in with government crisis personnel in stenciled wind-breakers with radio transmitters crackling and cell phones chiming. Family members of victims were beginning to show up with questions. Nobody asked Shale anything.

Shale's numb demeanor was broken by the entrance of a patrolman escorting a young woman with a pony tail, a ruffled pink skirt, a powder-blue blouse, knocked-off Lanvin ballet slippers and a green-and-yellow tattoo on her shoulder. A patrolman spoke to his superior: "Captain, this is Gretchen Sobieski. Says she might have information about our suspect."

Shale Gimmelfarb looked up from the table to behold a child in a pink and quivering garment. She was delicate and beautiful and sad and feminine. She was as tiny and helpless as a Starling chick. Her eyes were big and wet and Shale felt a fatherly and protective feeling for her in her obvious distress.

"Hello. I'm Captain Sal Giambelluca. What's your name?"

"Gretchen Sobieski." The poor thing could hardly look up when she spoke and she spoke almost inaudibly.

"Do you know somebody named Jupiter Mingo?"

"He's my boyfriend. He works here at the hotel. Do you know where he is?"

"Jupiter is dead," said the Captain. Shale kept his gaze fixed upon Gretchen as the Captain continued. "He was killed on the roof of this hotel. But not before he himself killed a whole platoon of police officers. Not before he killed even more innocent civilians. Jupiter Mingo is dead."

Shale looked around the table at the blanching

and swallowing officers from the New Orleans police force, the FBI agents, the representatives from Homeland Security and the Justice Department with their flaccid necks and closed mouths. Gretchen Sobieski, alone, stood erect and alert.

As he beheld the precious creature, Shale felt none of the usual scrofulous lechery that typically accompanied the sight of resplendent female youth. He saw in Gretchen Sobieski a beautiful and vulnerable sadness better left in its inviolable solitude. With his hand pressed against the blood-stained gauze taped on to his left flank, he watched Gretchen withdraw from the Moss dining room toward the St. Charles Avenue door of The Watercress as she vanished in the darkening air. He had nothing to say and so said nothing.

As members of the law enforcement contingent gathered their papers and equipment, Shale stood and began his walk through the kitchen to the employee porthole that led to Josephine Street. Into the twilight of an oblivious and ridiculous New Orleans, Shale Gimmelfarb, hungry at last for the bread of affliction, walked the few short blocks to Dryades Street where he would collect certain personal effects he had forgotten somewhere along the way to the hotel earlier that day.

- The End -